In Euphoria

Donna D. Vitucci

Rebel ePublishers
Detroit London

Rebel ePublishers
Detroit, Michigan 48223

All names, characters, places, and incidents in this publication are fictitious or are used fictitiously. Any resemblance to real persons, living or dead, events or locales is entirely coincidental.

ISBN-13: 978-1-944077-32-7
ISBN-10: 1-944077-32-4

Interior design by *Caryatid Design*

Portions of *In Euphoria* have appeared, in slightly different form, in the following publications:

In Euphoria, *Front Range Review*, Winter 2010
Someone Said Fail, *Chautauqua Literary Review*, Spring 2010

For David

She had been born with a face
that would let her get her way.

Bob Seger
Hollywood Nights

In Euphoria

Drought for three or four successive summers in Euphoria cracked creek bottoms and frogs died trying to wedge into those cracks. Tree roots staggered, their stress unremarkable. September churned the Midwest like a hurricane up from the Gulf, whipped Lake Michigan shallows to a froth that would top a tall man. Wheat and soybeans slanted across Missouri, Indiana, Ohio. Pine trees lifted, sent the ground's crust up, so their roots shivered the way their cones and needles would if the world hadn't upended.

Immediately, the pine tree leaning against power lines required attention, and Pauline called an SOS in to the electric company. They put her address in the queue.

Waiting, Pauline thought. On hold. Ain't that just perfect?

She drove to one of her favorite lingering places that had power: the Goodwill Store. At least her car had gas. The place was party-busy with people drawn out from the eerie shade all over town to mill about in the store's salvatory light.

"Power failure sucks," said some safety-pin-lipped teen

into her cell phone.

In the unisex aisle of hanging shirts, secluded from the entry and the front desk, Pauline mumbled that she preferred much-washed over new-scratchy. She wanted worn and lived in, a little broke down, she said.

Browsing the flannels there, too, Jared said, "I'm your man, then." His blurt-out sat like a toad between them on the floor.

Ever see a woman pet a toad? A woman that's not got much fear of the slimy would downright do it. Pauline did. And here's a fact: toads are dry, not wet or sticky. Sticky part's the tongue.

He traipsed with her to the checkout, his arms empty, his eyes skipping over the other shoppers. Those he nearly bumped might have suspected him high, but he wasn't. He was infused with possibility, channeling it, he was a live wire. He refrained from winking at an old man to whom he wanted to shout, "Look at the bargain I found."

Crumpling to her chest a plastic bag full of just-purchased old flannels so she could pocket her wallet, Pauline said she'd welcome company if he followed her on up the hill after he paid.

"I'm not buying, just looking," he said. Then trailing her in the parking lot, dividing toward their cars he said, "What'll we do?"

"Wait for the electric," she said.

"Yeah, sure," Jared said. "I'm in." He ducked into his driver's seat.

She had interest. It's how he could drive across the top of her lawn, and she'd excuse him. Not forgive, but she'd excuse, and still hail him to the porch instead of cussing him out. From splintery chairs there Jared watched with Pauline for the energy trucks, then observed the jump-suited men with power saws in their hydraulic buckets decimate the tree. The lines lifted, the power came back on, they heard the fridge inside kick-start. The yard looked flat and uninteresting without the tree wreck to anchor the eye.

He said, "We should cut and stack it, the wood."

"We will."

"Your husband here?"

"In a few."

"What, few hours?"

"Days."

"'Til then?"

"Just us mice." She faced the street with her talk, where she resided, merely a gravel turnoff from the rural route few traveled. "Mice all a-tatter," she said, "looking for a hidey hole." Expecting no one, she could afford to string out the night.

In form-fitting jeans and a blouse the color of heather nicely revealing her neck, she appeared not at all tattered to Jared. He craned this way and that in a show of looking around. She had never invited him so far before. Because yes, their Goodwill scene had been prepped and propped up for shoppers, observers, and diligent spies. This was not their first time. Jared said, "Damned secluded place."

She stood and said, "Care for a drink? We can dare open the fridge now." He went with her in to the dark house where night had fallen. He liked drinking in seclusion; he'd forgotten that but remembered it now. Pauline had a way of helping him remember.

She turned on the god-awful kitchen light, tingeing the windows green and their faces tallowy. "Welcome to my mark-down. Got it in a foreclosure. One man's tragedy, another man's treasure. Or in this case, a woman's. All on sale. I've been here a year."

"And I'm only seeing this now?"

"A man needs time to prove himself."

"You feel I have?"

The refrigerator light illuminated her face when she reached in for the drinks, while it increased the shadows under her eyes. Jared thought maybe she hadn't been sleeping so well lately.

He said, "Foolish, you up here all alone."

"You think so?"

He nodded. "Foolish waste."

She didn't blink. She could have, but she didn't. In fact, she longed to blink the dryness from her eyes. "Two months enough time to form this opinion?"

"Two times too much," he said. "I knew it in our first minute."

They went back outside with their beers and sat. He lit two cigarettes and passed her one.

She hooked her boot's instep on the lower porch rail, clunker boots from the seventies. He guessed a person could still find Frye boots, somebody's beat-up donations retrieved and cleaned by the resellers. They'd met, after all, in the Goodwill.

"You come up on my land for some clear reason?" Pauline said.

"Can't say."

"Why not?"

"Don't know yet if it's come to me, or I to it."

"The reason?"

"The clarity."

They enjoyed hiding behind their smartass talk.

He looked at her, a woman, stuck in intimidating boots. He'd had the shit kicked out of him before – body and soul, many a time blood brought to his face. Thought he'd seen the end of that, but when was there ever an end unless you holed up and died?

He was just going to put it to her. "I thought you invited me."

She smiled, and the porch then didn't even need its electric light. "I did. Indeed I did." She got up, reached one arm inside the screen door, and flipped off the switch. He identified her location by her cigarette and its smoke, and then the creak of the chair taking her weight.

The dark brought the trees to their elbows. Every woodsy animal sound was waiting to interrupt their porch talk.

"All my eggs are in one basket," she said.

He said, "I love eggs, and if I had to choose, I'd choose your half price half-dozen."

"Half price because they're second-hand?"

He didn't care if some other guy had been her first choice. He said, "We're all of us used."

Jared tilted his chair on its hind legs to reach the ledge and strike a match there. Again the woods telescoped the two of them. Even the night birds shut their songs in their throats. He watched the fire until he had to drop it, and he'd bet she'd been watching it too, because her leg stretched out toward him, long in those jeans. Her clompy boot sole covered what was already extinguished.

"He's got a name," she said.

Jared tensed.

"Tom," she said.

"You know, it's odd, you're married and all, but your honesty comes from some deeper place."

Her laugh knifed and missed. "Deeper than marriage?" she said, "He wouldn't think so."

"'Course he's not where your honesty's directed."

Her lips pursed to quit the smile, and he saw he'd made a bit of an inroad with her where he hadn't managed before.

"I can see why people flirt with you, flit to you. You draw them. Hell, girls, too. I saw the chick at the Goodwill ringing you. They're all moths when they get near you. You and your light."

The talk about light, he meant it. She had gold in her hair, if she wanted evidence. He wasn't about to churn up small bits of truth into flattery that might take her out at the knees. He wanted their trading to be honest. But he also didn't know shit about her. He'd like to remedy that. He'd like to hug her knees, and then have her plant them by his shoulders the way he knew she could.

She'd been hungry for talk like his, interest like his, investment directed straight and primary at her. She hadn't recognized this lack until she met him, but she sure knew it now.

He said, "Don't you need to eat? I could take us to town for a bite."

"Or I could throw something together," she said.

So she intended he stay. She'd give him rope to hang himself, and he'd enjoy the asphyxiation. But maybe she was looking for nothing but company until her man pulled up. In a couple of days, she'd said.

"Supper," he said. Simple, declarative, not even a sentence, just a word, an agreement. They tripped inside. His boot snagged the toe strip and he fell into her and she steadied him. Not what he would have planned, but it worked. She smelled of pine; the whole place did, inside and out, as if the workmen had split the tree in the front doorway.

Again that gruesome kitchen light. Jared looked around

for candlesticks, a kerosene lantern, anything to wipe the hard look from both of them.

From a lower cabinet, she dragged out an electric contraption.

"Panini maker," she said, brandishing it like she was going to brain him. "From the Goodwill."

He said, "I would have used a plain old skillet. Also from the Goodwill."

They locked eyes over the bread she buttered.

Once the panini started cooking the whole place smelled greasy and warm. Their bellies growled. She laughed, then he did. He twisted open two more beers from the mildly cold fridge, held hers for her while she flipped the sandwich. The bread crisped, they toasted. Their teeth clicked in kissing. They split apart, she split the sandwich, her fingers trembly, but good trembly. He brought his half to her mouth and she bit. Cheese oozed onto her chin. He had to lick it. The two of them kissed and chewed, kissed and chewed, swallowed it all down, the beers empty. They stood at the beginning of being filled.

"That was the last of the bread," she said. She shrugged, hopeful, and eager not to betray it. She'd learned to guard what she had.

He grabbed her oily fingers and took her down the hallway, unsure where the bedroom was, but he led her through the dark while she directed him from behind. They worked together, they just did, and it was nothing like work.

"Here," she said. "Right here." She stumbled into him the way he'd run into her on first coming into the house.

Next to her bedroom closet door, she'd set an old full-length mirror, another thrift store find. Nothing fancy, with its two tarnished corners and chewed-at maple frame that had once been quite fine before it graced strangers' attics. The piece lost its cheval frame before it crossed into Pauline's hands, so she leaned it there against the wall. During her walks around the bedroom while she brushed her teeth, bending to peek out the window, toothbrush shoved inside her cheek, and circling back to the sink, in the mirror her shadow appeared first, anticipating her form.

"You see yourself coming and going," Tom would say, a gentle dig at her narcissism. Those were during better times, when her shadow scouted the trail and beckoned she should follow. Show up soon, the shadow said, good things ahead. Or maybe Tom was who said that. With Jared in her bed, the shadows doubled. His and Pauline's played in that mirror like fairies in Shakespeare's woods; they made asses out of themselves and giggled over it. And then, as if the mirror and its reflections teetered in the long-lost cheval, they cradled and were cradled, they rocked and were rocked.

In the morning the chainsaw revved. Jared needed only to turn in Pauline's bed to see out the window his lover in the yard putting blade to the smaller tree arms. He fell back to her pillow and the roar of the machine. It was that good, that deafening, it erased every place and person and predicament. He woke a second time to voices mumbling in another room.

Jared's hangover didn't allow for his best judgment. He entered the kitchen, searching out a huge cold drink. It couldn't have been worse if he'd stood there naked and scratching his balls.

Pauline had wood chips in her hair. She said, "We have

company," a bemused smile on her lips.

"You could have worn some pants, man," said the company.

Jared shrugged and felt himself shrink inside his boxers. "She told me to make myself at home."

"Sure, blame Pauline," she said. The day called for juggling.

The company—with no introductions Jared still knew it was Tom, so he thought of him as Tom – Tom claimed everything within eyeshot, spread his arm in a motion of largesse. "Mi casa, su casa, eh?"

They were nowhere near the border. They were in white bread Midwest, southeast of Champagne, in a place called Euphoria.

"Spare me the Spanish," Jared said.

"Where do you get off talking like that in my place?"

Jared kept his mouth shut.

Tom said, "Look around, Pauline. What haven't I given you?"

For a fierce woman, she turned misty-eyed on a dime. She narrowed that mist at the kitchen table. "What I didn't know I didn't have."

"Which is?"

"You wouldn't understand."

"Try me."

She squirmed, and when she squirmed Jared found her only more lovely. "I can't give name to it," she said.

Tom said, "Bullshit," his boil nudging the surface.

Interloper Jared started backing out.

"You," Tom shouted, finger pointing, shaking in its point. "You go nowhere."

"I'm just getting my pants," he said, to which Tom whirly-gigged his hand in permission. In the bedroom

Jared wanted to spin out, take down the whole top of Pauline's bureau, her knick-knacks, the mirror, her keepsakes, all of it dusted in the particular array she'd imposed, but he held back the need to destroy. For two months they'd been keeping things cool, and it looked like now they'd slipped. Or maybe it was time for truth.

Jared had a knife he resisted using. That had been a promise of his – no more emotion-fueled action. Examine things first, he'd pledged, and the source of his emotion, and his emotion with Pauline – he couldn't get a grasp on that. She was quicksilver, dazzling and elusive. Getting ready to dress, he swung around his jeans, a little too angry about mercurial Pauline, and his big Texas-bought belt buckle hit and shattered the window.

"Fuckin' A," someone shouted from outside the bedroom.

"We see eye to eye on things," he heard her tell Tom.

And Tom's, "Bullshit. You don't know this joker. Name one thing you see eye to eye on if that's so god-all important to you."

Jared's fingers hovered before pulling up his zipper, but Pauline had no comment.

"See?" said Tom. "All's you're agreeing on is your two asses in one bed."

So wrought up in argument, they hadn't heard Jared bust the glass, but he removed enough not to cut as he slipped out to level ground.

In passing her car, he noted her license plate, DOV569, and he stabbed himself with memories of the many times he'd followed "the dove," as he called her, to some trysting place.

Pauline was just another thing in his life he wanted and he wasn't going to have.

Pauline, his lay, his love, his lovey-dovey dove, his feathered lightning, his silver bullet. A good twenty years ago, Jared's army-bound brother, Sten, took him to summer skeet practice in prep for his first official dove hunt in a mowed-down cornfield. Sten, who ended up in Afghanistan, lost in the poppies.

"Just remember," he told Jared, "clays fly straight but doves juke all over the goddamn sky."

And, "The longer you track a dove, the greater chance you'll slow or stop your swing or the bird'll dodge off. Instead, think *eyes to the target, hands to the target,* in that order. Lock your eyes on the dove as it comes to you, but don't budge the gun until you're ready to shoot." Then he told Jared, "On a short lead, pretend the bird has a dollar bill in its beak. Lock on the dove's head, hands and the gun will follow. Just get the muzzle out in front and good things will happen."

Short lead, long lead, so much to remember. "Then what's a dove when it comes at you from overhead?" Jared said. He took a guess. "No lead, right?"

Sten said, "A dove overhead looks farther away than it really is, just like the moon's huge when it's touching the horizon but seems smaller and smaller as it climbs up the sky." Jared tried to slice his thoughts into steps one, two, and three, but Sten had overflowed the afternoon with his know-it-all talk. No boy of eleven, already awestruck, could hold onto so much new news.

The doves streaked by with their eyes and their throttles wide open, a stream of tiny gray bullets zipping overhead. They came in at every conceivable angle and flared wildly once Sten started firing, and yelling.

"Swing the gun with the bird, and when it disappears behind the muzzle, shoot! Just blot it out, pull the trigger, and keep swinging!"

The bird folded clean like an envelope and took forever to fall to the ground.

Sten said, "Did you watch where it fell? Did you track and identify something to mark the place?"

"I shot it, isn't that enough? Jeez."

Sten spat into the field and his words reduced Jared and the whole day's worth of glory, "No point in shooting birds you can't recover."

"And where do you think you're going?" Tom called from the cast-open front door. Pauline peered over his shoulder, visoring her eyes with one beautiful hand, locating Jared in the far-off.

I'm right here, babe, he wanted to say. Arm's length. Just reach out your arm. Jared had stopped and, with little to no thought, had been running his key along the side panel of Pauline's car, gouging thin lines in the paint. Blue had not been this old Bonneville's first color.

If he couldn't walk away with Pauline, what was the point in walking at all? He froze, as though he'd been frozen among the corn stalk stubble, stunned by all the little gray rockets exploding around him, and stilled by the fact that in the midst of sound and flight and gunshot and Sten's nagging, he'd managed to pluck one unlikely dove from the stratosphere. He tracked Pauline behind Tom on the porch. He wasn't going to miss where she landed. Hell, he'd help her land, he'd cushion her landing, he'd offer up the soft parts of his body to her, to the dry earth, to whatever Tom tried jabbing between them.

Jared said, "You two got things to settle, obviously." He returned his car keys to his pants pocket beside the knife.

Tom took a step. "And you don't think you're part of that? You're the instigator, you're the reason and the goddamn rhyme."

Normally a little spitfire, Pauline caved in. She stood, quiet, on the porch with her hands wrapped around her ribs. Tom squashed her spirit, anybody with eyes could see that. He was a good-looking man. Hell, if Jared were her, he probably wouldn't leave him either.

Behind Tom, Pauline rolled the sleeves of one of the flannel shirts she'd bought yesterday up to her elbows. She said, "What can you do when you love somebody but follow?" Jared heard that where he idled beside her car and it twisted his gut.

Tom said, "You, Pauline. Not me, you. Christ, at least own your tramping around." "Okay," she whispered, and her whisper rose above the trees weakened by drought, all those poised to still falter and crash. "I love someone, somebody else." Him, she thought, unable to curb her glance to the driveway.

Tom looked at her as if she'd just fired a gun in his belly. Hurting him, really tearing him up, she could see – exactly what she'd been avoiding these last months. But now the hurting snaked through her house, it shed its skin on her land, and she saw things could get worse, and that they would. She felt sick to her stomach.

Jared turned from her car and headed back to the house because while he'd been waiting, he'd also been mulling the sweet times, such as when he'd confessed to Pauline that, "God brought you to me."

She said, "So you could complicate my life?" They already lay in his bed, fast upon that first meeting, it happened that way between them, explosive.

"So I could love you," he said.

"You mean so you could be loved."

He'd smiled where they lay in the dark, and he knew

she knew the grin taking over the features of his face. "Same circuit, us, our one big love."

His feelings for Pauline were concentrated like gunpowder under the packing rod in an old rifle. The kick in his stride scattered gravel. He fingered the handle of his knife. It wanted to leap from his pocket and he clutched it to keep it hidden from the two on the porch.

"You talk to her like that and I'll be making you quit," he said.

Tom said, "Today, you think?"

The self-satisfied jerk, practiced at baiting because he probably did it all day long to Pauline. Tom worked a number on her, and she let him – out of love or fear or obligation, didn't matter why to Jared, who wanted to deck the bastard.

Jared plucked a dove out of the sky with his eyes closed, he'd gotten plain perfect since the first shaky days in corn stubble with Sten. He wouldn't need any short lead, long lead shit with Tom. Tom was like the moon on the horizon, or a tin can set on Pauline's porch rail, begging to be picked off.

The three of them stood together like triplets, a lopsided triangle of flannel.

Tom laughed and chopped his hand in the air so Pauline ducked and Jared flinched and scooted to her in the same one move. He smothered his impulse to deck Tom.

"Don't fear me, honey," Tom said. "I was just going to say, look at us dressed the same, like the three bears – papa, mama and baby bear." He took on the gruff voice, "Someone's been sleeping in my bed." Then a lazy-daisy voice, "Oh, someone 's been sleeping in my bed." And finally falsetto baby, "Someone's been sleeping in my bed."

He swung around in a circle and nailed Jared with a push to the chest. "And there he is!"

Jared wasn't leaving Pauline with this guy.

"Rethinking it now," Tom said, "maybe you should go."

Jared looked at her; truth was he never stopped looking at her. "Pauline?" She shook her head, which could mean I don't know, don't ask me, go, or don't go.

"I told you before, the only one who can make me quit you is you," Jared said.

He had said that, she'd heard it and felt it as true and insistent then as it rang through her now.

Tom said to him, "Can't you see you're not wanted here?"

Jared, with his eyes boring into her, willed Pauline to speak. Her lips parted, but then she turned to swat at cobwebs trailing from the porch eaves.

"For me to believe, she'll need to say it."

Tom got belligerent. "I said it, and that's enough for all of us."

Sten used to say, "There'll always be a gun, but the knife is a sign of who you are." His brother taught Jared the need to carry the blade and lean it into someone if necessary. Tom didn't look the type for weapons, more likely to call the law than to vigilante Jared off. Off Pauline's place.

Jared said, "Doesn't she have something to say, this being hers?"

"What's hers is mine," Tom said.

In Tom appropriating Pauline and what she had acquired on her own, Jared felt like a bullet slipped into a chamber, that chamber being his gut. He was in his own gut, if that made any sense. Not shooting, not shot at, but loaded to shoot, he was the thing inside, the projectile, the source of a wound. Like the doves, he could take this guy way inside the box, would never need the amount of ammo retailers averaged for misfires.

He had the neck of Tom's shirt bunched inside his fist, lifting the guy off the ground.

Pauline stomped and the boards emitted dust. "Will you two quit before I call the law and have you both hauled off my property?"

Tied up the way he was, Tom still managed to taunt, "When'd you get so gutsy?"

Jared said, "She's her own self, always has been."

"True," Tom said. He twisted in Jared's grip so as to claim her with a look across the porch. "You're my gutsy Pauline, right, baby?"

Jared had to haul him a little higher, and strangle him for that. Pauline made him forget the things he'd been – the sad, the spoiled, the failed, the bitter. How dare Tom fuck with that?

Pauline said, "Why don't you both piss on me and get it over with, marking your property like a couple of goddamned dogs?"

Tom had been flailing for balance, but mostly sucking air. Jared had been off in his own space, so inside his gut and what his gut was telling him to do, it was like Mission Control had hold of him and he was just robotic arms and legs doing the grunt work on an airless planet. He had to remind himself to breathe. See his talent in walling off part of his mind so he could perpetrate crime? Something a person taking up with Jared would have to watch out for. With so many arms, he was an octopus, he held Tom with one, withdrew the knife from his pocket with another, and with a third, he planned grabbing and making off with

Pauline. But no third arm, no dream, and she wasn't budging from her porch step anyway.

Her eyes, intent on Jared's, telegraphed, "Let him go. Or I'll never."

Why couldn't she just say it?

Hurting Tom would earn Jared another reject check on the tally board he imagined hung in Pauline's mind, where she evaluated the pros and cons of him. Jared would give her no reason to push him away. If they broke, it wouldn't be over anything he'd done. It'd be because they'd made plans she couldn't see her way through to completing.

Jared loosed his grip, let the knife fall to the bottom of his pocket, down deep, almost to his knee. He looked straight at Pauline and said, "Help is here if you want it."

She put her hand to her mouth – he thought she might cry, Jesus – but then she went chewing at a hangnail, one of her several lovable bad habits. She might as well have been gnawing on his middle.

No knife, no fight, no pain. Except for the hole in his gut, Jared curled around as he turned to walk down and away from the porch.

"Where're you going?" Pauline called. Had her failing nerve killed everything?

"Let him run," Tom said.

Jared zeroed in on the gravel scuffling up under his boot soles and the birds quieting in the afternoon heat of maybe one of the last good autumn days. He could practically feel the grass growing its final inch, the leaves crisping and roasting and breaking their connections.

Tom said, "Things will be different, Pauline."

She said, "Your promises aren't worth the paper they're writ on."

Almost two years see-sawing with Tom, she'd gotten

well acquainted with dodgy commitment and how he'd try to otherwise slide free of his promises. She bought this place, on her own, during one of his flights of fancy, and damn if she didn't lead him back through its front door, just like she was doing now. She didn't know why she did half the things she did. Jared turned from the hurtful glare of their porch disappearance, gripped the door handle of his Pontiac. Old friend, old flirt, cool and alive under his touch. The way Pauline had been.

He winced at his inability to not think of her, got in and kicked it.

He reversed and twisted the coupe a couple times this way and that, reorienting down the gullied gravel slope, only to realize parts of the pine tree Pauline had been slicing up earlier blocked his exit. He gunned the motor, thinking he'd just drive over the lawn, how she'd cuss him for that. Then he jerked the gear into park, killed the engine.

It took twenty minutes to move the untouched limbs the power company brought down into the deeper grass and stack what wood she'd made manageable. This he could do for her, she'd know it for the symbol it was. They were always talking shit like that, conjuring stand-ins for their feelings, tokens, jokes and stories that said one thing and ferried deeper, personal, between-them-two meaning, all the unsaid. He thought they'd seen eye to eye, but he'd misinterpreted her sneaking out to him again and again. Their symbol wasn't fire, it was smoke. He worked sweat over the downed tree, and now he was smelling himself, himself and Pauline mixed on his skin. Shit, he hadn't showered or got breakfast, brunch or lunch. He didn't even guzzle that big glass of water he'd been thirsting for when he first walked into the kitchen.

He was ready to fly the hell down off this hill.

And so inside his car, he began the rumbly descent along the gravel.

Pauline jack-in-the-boxed in the backseat, straddle-leaped the console and sat opposite him, she his one big escape dream, her hair mussed, her face brimming with her stowaway secret.

"Let's hightail it outta this town, partner," she said, all wicked eye and grin.

The Pontiac fishtailed when Jared punched the brakes. He kept them out of the main road, but it was a less-traveled road anyway. He let the engine idle.

"I'm apart when I don't know when I'll see you again," Jared said.

"Apart from what?"

"In parts, parted from you, in pieces, you know what I mean."

Pauline concentrated on her clasped hands gracing her thighs as Jared spoke, which pretty much hid her face from him behind her hair. She grabbed at the luscious stuff, one-handed, the way she did to cinch it back in the midst of sex, because she wore it loose for him to enjoy. Then she let it fall, the highlights in the brown reminding Jared how precious she was to him. Gold, gem, jewel precious.

He would not allow her to blindside him. "Tom knows about us now. You're fooling yourself if you believe he'll leave us on our own."

"So let's go."

"Nope."

"What do you mean nope?"

"If you're coming with me, then you're going to leave him straight under his nose, none of this slinking off. He doesn't know you're with me, am I right?"

"You know you are."

He nodded, and the simple flick induced a headache. "I'm past that, Pauline. You leave him for me, you do it in the open, make a statement. Show your cards to him and to me."

"I'm not game playing."

"I know you're not, baby, but you have to come clean, mostly to yourself."

"But I don't know how."

God, but she could make even whining sound pretty.

Jared said, "That's it then, ain' it? You got to go?"

She looked hopeful and helpless with her hair falling in her eyes. "Go with you."

Jared shook off that idea. "Not 'til you tell Tom to his face and I witness the telling."

He might as well have told her to grow another head.

He said, "Get out."

She stared at him and in that stare Jared had never seen her more open, more available, like a field awaiting seed, but he turned and watched the speedometer consistently register zero while he gunned the gas.

He wouldn't say why and she wouldn't ask, and finally he heard her click the door open, heard the rustle of her sweet bottom off the seat and out of his vehicle. She shut the door quietly, didn't slam it in her usual way. Denying her took him right outside himself, as if he were standing with Pauline on that side of the Pontiac's passenger door. He was fucking split in two, and reveling in the split feeling.

She stood with her hand on the chrome edge of the open window and so it was up to him to drive.

It tore him up to leave her, but when his flayed edges stopped hissing in the breeze of Wennert Ridge Road, they felt not like rips, but flutters, like promises, like soothing hands; his own hands calming the gallop of his heart, or the hands of God or an angel, hands of his angel, lovey-dovey Pauline.

"Wings of a dove," Sten would have said. "Sounds pretty but they're just a means for whittling your sight down the barrel of a gun. On opening day there are plenty of young and semi-dumb birds around."

Jared didn't want nubile or dizzy, he wanted crackerjack-smart Pauline.

He heard Sten urge, "Lighten up and open up then. Doves have an airy, easily broken bone structure."

Jared nearly rolled the Pontiac, righted it, pulled to the berm once he got free of the blind curve he'd been cruising. He ran his arm across his eyes and let the flannel shirt sleeve absorb his perspiration. His heart hammered a different beat from the ticking of the car's underside. Did he want to break Pauline? No, he did not. But. He knew the way back to her place, as private and secluded as any sheltered ambush where he might blend in with her familiar horizon until it was too late for her to juke off to Tom. Waking with her in her very own bedroom had been a start he was in no way prepared to ditch. He wanted to rest amid her brilliance; he wanted to reflect her light.

Stupid talk of bird-in-the-sky memories, and planets and stars. You're either on this earth, or you're under it—an email from Sten before he'd vanished that burned constant in Jared's brain. Pauline would fly, when the time was right, directly at him, and she might not even know it was him she was swifting to; maybe he'd decoy her into it, "but that'd be okay," Sten said, and Jared sensed his brother was right, as long as Pauline ended up in his arms where he'd otherwise be clutching a gun.

And Further

To backtrack – what Pauline once viewed as pitched, pleased-for love now appeared hot grease poured down the sink, bound to gummy up the works.

How Tom was good to her. She thought she owed him a review of his fine points. Which were? One, he cut up grapefruit so it sat in a bowl in the fridge, waiting for her sleepy mouth, her lolling tongue. That was sweet. But grapefruit season in Euphoria was so abbreviated as to hardly count.

Two, his endearments. Pauline babe, he called her. But then everybody called her babe. It might as well be her middle name.

"Scooch on over to my side, Pauline babe," he'd say in bed. "My wild side," he'd say, all Lou Reed-ish. He'd worn black eyeliner like Lou when she reconnected with him post-high-school – a pose that passed quickly. Not in calendar time, but relationship time. If he dressed in a suit, you might take Tom for a banker, but he was no white-collar worker. His closet sheltered denim, flannel, leather, and used up cotton. He'd been the one taught Pauline the good of Goodwill. There, Point Three in his favor.

"You can get a decent suit at Goodwill," she told him. He avoided formal wear. Thing is, every notch on his side of the column could also be inked beside Jared. Jared shopped Goodwill – hell, he acted like he invented the idea of re-use. Pennies for a tee shirt, dollars for a coat. Thrifty or cheap, didn't matter; the guy aimed for quality. He said, "That's why I'm pursuing you, Pauline."

Pauline and Tom had been hitched going on two years, their sticking with the marriage as much a surprise to them as to anyone. She had no business drawing sides to choose, or dividing her love. She should have put on blinders to focus purely on Tom, whom she knew from growing up in the same neighborhood. They rode bikes with the same group of kids in sixth or seventh grade, nothing diary-worthy. One beat-up September afternoon during this youthful time, Tom invited her into his house for a slug of Gatorade.

"You big dummy," Tom's dad said. "Left the goddamn fridge door open." He railed on right in front of Pauline, who could have been a girlfriend. She wasn't, but she could have been.

Clueless old man, putting Tom down in front of a thirsty, wind-whipped stranger.

Tom's little sister, Fiona, stood in the hallway, about seven years old and sucking an orange popsicle, taking in her brother's faults and the man who named them, probably swearing when she grew up she'd never let Daddy call her *dummy* in front of her boyfriends. Fee blew out the day she turned sixteen, tromped like Pauline in similar uneven roaming, stepped in the prints Pauline had pressed in mud with clunker Frye boots. Fiona fell in with her band, hooked up with her guitar man, seduced him right out from under Pauline.

Years later, when Tom and Pauline wed, the old man and Tom's stepmom, Maudie, said, "Finally our Tommy's got a girl he can keep."

Thing is, Pauline wasn't a woman for keeping, for keeps, or to be kept.

She'd traveled first for ten years with an almost-made-it band before running into Tom at Eli's Lounge, a bit of higher ground in the middle of Euphoria.

With the band sound-checking amid shadows, the lead singer parted his hair in front of a cracked mirror as Tom and Pauline spied each other all grown up and ordering drinks. She raised an eyebrow and he lifted his, added a wry I-think-I-know-you smile. She almost laughed aloud when she saw he wore eyeliner, but then she remembered how he smelled all weedy following a hot afternoon of biking the hills, and the eyeliner didn't squash the scent she was surprised to discover lodged in her memory bank. She could imagine his shirt bunched into a roll of soft fabric where he'd tucked it in, the way he did as a boy. She nearly set her palm on his low back to verify. They stayed beside their full glasses, and one another, at the bar.

"Fridge still open?" she said.

Tom said, "What?"

"Oh, never mind. It was a dumb cast-back to the past."

He had perfect teeth, which he showed her. "You don't look a day over twenty, Pauline." She barked outrageous private glee, then covered her mouth with her hand to stop stupid stuff from escaping, but stupid escaped anyway.

"I've had plenty of unrequited."

"Ha. This I sincerely doubt, girl. Name one."

"Neal Boneker."

Tom's eyes lit up.

She added, "For the stage, he shortened it to Bone."

"You and Neal Bone?" He cut his attention to the stage, frontman still absent, and then riveted back to her.

Pauline nodded. She had a story prepared, a true story.

"Those crocked audience members calling out 'give us a Bone,' and 'hey, Boner,' holding aloft their cell phones, all eerie glowing. Him perched on a stool like a troubadour, laughing drunk right along with. He called them the masses, and I couldn't help but think back to church the Catholics did while me and my friends scuffed into Sunday School in the Methodist Annex."

She took to the road with Neal, did the band's cooking. "Yes," she said, "like arranging catering and the before-gig buffet. More like jiggling a pan over a campfire. The Neal Bone Band never elbowed out of the low tier gigs. Honest, sometimes night was sleeping bag in the back of the van."

For the boys, she stewed dandelion greens and brewed dandelion wine. The band loved her, they kissed her bare shoulder, but only Neal did she allow to lift the strap of the undershirt she wore and kiss that sheltered strip of skin, too. The others loved her like a sister. Neal loved her blind.

She told Tom, "I sued him when he left."

Tom said, "You two have papers filed at the courthouse?"

"Lord, no." That touched her then, a man caring about messing in another guy's marriage.

"Common law?"

"Nothing so much as. Just unpaid income, earned fair and square, that my wallet never saw."

Tom nodded. "Sure, a girl needs her funds."

"Her fun?"

"Funds, I said."

She hit his forearm, resting on the bar between them. "I know. I'm joshing." She sighed and drank the rest of her beer, felt all hands and feet and useless yammer.

Tom signaled to the bartender to bring another round.

"Yup," she said. "Band got paid, roadies got paid. But Neal tended to think, I guess, loving was good enough for all I gave." She stared into the far-off. "What I gave." Paused, all dreamy and morose, then said, "Fuck that."

Tom said, "I hear ya."

They clinked beer mugs and drank big.

She nodded away the rest of the narration, the boring part, the decline every good thing brings with it.

Boner took the stage and they both turned their bar stools to face the band. She hadn't seen him in almost a year; he still looked willowy, still made her veins rise close to her skin. The music crashed around the room and Pauline endured the familiarity – a big hum of angry bees. She closed her eyes and leaned into Tom, and hoped Neal saw, but she knew he got so inside his head when he sang he might as well be on another planet. She felt stung.

Tom spoke over-loud into her ear, "I'm not blowing smoke, babe."

Drowsy, and half-drunk, she pitched a little more into him. It was an easy slide from there.

Tom's folded knees, as they later lay in bed together, formed a shelf for Pauline to sit on, horizontally. She snuggled in, keepsake on his shelf, and felt change about to rumble through. She held a mouthful of evolution. She thought she was tasting organic matter, and believed organic was good, but it was sick coming up over her teeth. Her and Tom in the bathroom then, street ghosts at the bubble-glass window. He reached for the wall switch and she hit him in the thigh, as she knelt and he stood. "No." Moaned so you'd think a little light would kill her.

Wintertime, still he slid open the window.

"Here," he said, passing her a towel for her mouth, and a glass of water she dared not drink. She swished around a gulpful and spat into the toilet, collapsed on her heels with her arms draping the cold tub edge.

Tom set an open sweater at the back of her neck to cover part of her nakedness, patted her shoulder. How many guys owned a cardigan? All the good dads on TV wore sweaters – Mr. Douglas, Ward, Bill-Cosby-Huxtable. Alongside woozy in her head, she also had this thought: She'd been tenuous, and rootless. By sleeping with Fiona, Neal had cauterized the tendrils Pauline had allowed herself to place in him. Neal would call them hooks. Well, fuck Neal. Now Tom filled her whole blurry vision. He couldn't help it if he was Fiona's brother.

Tom knelt with her next to the toilet, and when he lifted her chin Pauline jerked aside.

"My breath smells like death," she said.

He laughed. "How do you know?"

"Tastes like it."

"I'll decide."

"No."

"No?"

"No."

He closed in on her, wrestling, laughing, angling for kissing but she clamped shut her lips. Then more sick erupted on the tiny tiled floor. With paper towels, he wiped the mess, dumped it in the kitchen trash.

On his return, she said, "I don't always lose my shit like this."

Tom stepped naked in front of her into the tub and tugged her up by her hand. He said, "I liked you pretty, Pauline, and I'm liking you still."

His sweater fell off her. She used him for balance under

the shower as they washed away the sick smell and made themselves sober.

She thought of a line from one of Neal's songs: *Smoke, smolder, rest and run.* She guessed she and Tom had reached the end of that string. She wasn't one to sit still with acceptance; she could admit this.

Keepsake means acquired, she later described to Tom's dad.

She visited the old man where Tom didn't bother. Tom, who was growing out of everything like a teenager in his second growth spurt – out of his dad, out of his jeans, out of his wife, Pauline.

"Out of complacency," she guessed he would say if she dogged him about it.

"See? I didn't bail first," she whispered.

Now she visited the old man and his wife. Woman was in the Alzheimer's wing, hadn't a clue. Pauline saved up her charms for men. She was simply wired that way. Hollis would not remember what she said to him, was well on his way to joining wispy-haired Maudie in the Forgetful Unit. He could remind Pauline how he cussed at Tom over tires rotated wrong in 1986, but he wouldn't remember her confidences.

She told Hollis, "Maybe sounds like I loved Neal more than I ever loved Tom." But Pauline did not compare lovers. Each one was a new knife in a drawer, different blades for different kinds of cutting. And man, but they sliced her up good, to ribbons.

A dream she had begun and then abandoned: children. At

thirty a woman begins considering what's out of her grasp, things she'd always believed would be. The babies she might have had, she thought of them as round balls of clay. They could grow to be anything – firemen, acrobats, gas station attendants, teachers, mommies and daddies, or they could run away with the circus. All the pretty hopes she had for them. But first, they had to *be*. She wasn't about to plead them down from heaven into their little car seats. Already she begged too much for what she never seemed to get. Neither Neal nor Tom seemed to know what she craved, which was she wanted their topmost love, to be their first consideration.

And had she laid out for tally purposes the story about the dog? Pendleton, a gorgeous shepherd-lab mix, with some red in him even, with a beautiful coat she brushed and brushed, the dog leaning back into her legs, smiling his doggy grin, eyes closed in ecstasy.

"Will you quit with that fucking dog?" Tom yelled out the front door. She had to brush Pen in the grass because Tom complained of shedding.

"Shorthairs do not shed," she said. "And whatever he's got in him, they're both short." Tom flipped his hand in the air, the way he did the time Jared tried stepping forward to protect her on the porch, a motion she interpreted as he couldn't be bothered.

She'd led Pendleton by his collar onto the lawn. She loved him there, cared for him there.

They were a twosome more than she and Tom were a twosome.

Tom maybe had a bad incident as a boy with a large dog. He never let up once she brought that dog home from the rescue. Pendleton was the bone Tom kept gnawing; he left it alone and then returned to set in more teeth marks.

Tom had terrific teeth. He bleached to make them pearlier. For a guy, he managed to fuss over a few personal details, which suggested to Pauline he was stepping out, but covering better.

He took Pen to get fixed and Pauline thought they'd turned a corner. But then he complained to her from the vet's when presented with the bill. "Didn't want him knocking up some bitch's bitch. We'd be having your ass sued."

Tom worried about lawsuits.

Pauline could name the time and place her life changed. Along the lot that fronted New Bethany Pentecostal, they'd set in some spanking new concrete. On her usual walk, Pauline had approached this new construction and the mystery of it.

Tom called it "the sidewalk to nowhere," a quarter mile the paver had set from the gravel drive leading back to the church. Where it dropped into a gully of sticks and gravel and shredded cellophane, stood a man wearing a scuffed suede jacket, with inches-long stitching across the back as if the coat had been in a knife fight. Too warm a day, especially for suede. The coat observation settled weirdly in Pauline's belly, made her consider the guy might not be all there upstairs and un-phased by weather; or a vagrant with everything he had draping his shoulders. They met where the sidewalk stopped and the rutted ground took over. She tried to detour, but he prevented her pass-thru. Her hands were empty; she didn't even carry a purse.

"I've been waiting for you," he said.

She had a buzzing in her ears and sweat in her hair. Next, she expected he'd reach out and grab her to keep her from running and he did and that was good because she would have run.

Right then she would have run.

"What do you want with me?"

"What do *you* want?" he said.

The way his eyes watched her she felt he could open up her head and look inside, tinker around, rewire her, sew her shut, and when he left she'd be a soulless robot with some kind of absolute current keeping her running. She wrestled out of his grasp, her arms suddenly chilled, the way women sometimes feel when they're frozen out from their own selves. Jared shed his coat and made her wear it. Above them the sun was blazing.

"Will you come with me?" he said.

"No," she said, but she stepped with him along the unpaved ground.

They said other things while they walked, like where was home and who the fuck are you, and have you been stalking me, and what does this mean.

And then she recalled having seen him at the Goodwill.

"This is my stop," she said. They stood in front of New Bethany.

"You were on your way to church?" He sported a disbelieving smile.

"It's possible." She needed to step inside or she feared taking more from him than his coat. Then he'd expect more, and she had no extra. All her goods were locked up with Tom.

She gestured at the building. "This is my destination."

"Nah. It's your beginning."

She laughed at this just-met Jared, supposing, like Tom, that he knew her. They did *not* know, none of them knew. She sat on a bench in New Bethany, thankful for hard furniture and solitude, and yes, even for God, though she had to guess at Him. Jared was gone when she stepped out later. She wore his coat home.

She volunteered thereafter to bring the church's collected donations to the Goodwill Store, carried them in piecemeal to increase her trips and her chances of running into Jared, which she did, each time. They'd walk next door to Burger King for a Coke, and then stroll around outside until their straws stirred only sweet crushed ice. A month of this made Pauline crazy. Craziness ruled.

"The last time I loved," Jared said, "I promised I'd never get so deep again." He paused and waited and she waited with him. "Leave and you'll kill me," he said.

She ignored his warnings because they stood on a visible street corner, waiting for a "walk" light, because they hardly knew each other then and men always exaggerated their misgivings to Pauline. She brought it out in them.

"Thinking of you sealing yourself off that way, it just breaks my heart," she said.

"Standing still is worse."

"You think I've settled?"

"I do."

"You don't know me.'"

"I'd work to change that."

In some ways, he sounded like a hired hand in a job interview, desperate for some around-the-house chore, any reason to draw near, any cause to catch a good meal. But then he brought her to his place and fed her and she saw he had more food than he needed, that he was dying to give what he had.

He repeated his claim from when they first met. "I've been waiting for you."

He ran his hand up the back of her neck, dug his fingers into her hair until he held her skull. He brought her forehead to his forehead, and she thought nothing could override this moment but water. It'd have to be a goddamn tsunami to change their course. They rubbed brow on brow, ground the bones there until it pained and then they did more.

They carried on like this the rest of the summer, whenever Tom's rig was assigned a cross-country route.

"How convenient, all this cross-continent travel," Pauline said. She said it like a complaint, while inside her vital organs lifted over where she'd go next, to whom, and how soon.

"Hey, I got to fucking work," Tom said.

That stung, because Pauline did not.

"Hey, I own this land and the house that sits on it, the house you call home, mister." That was her bargaining chip, her big gun. Tom wouldn't leave – he had a warm bed, and a woman in it, and a place to park his wheels until the phone gave him a new address to fly to. She'd have to kick him out if she ever wanted to bring Jared here. She didn't have the first idea how. She quit dreaming. She almost quit sleeping. But she did not quit Jared. Her concealments grew sloppy, maybe.

She recalled her first time with Tom, when he held her shoulders tightly in the shower, his fingers rubbery on her as he told her, "I want to show you how I can love you." A confounding wonder, as this sounded so much like Jared. Tom's intensity then had been a drug.

Now Jared was her connection.

She popped up out of her lover's bed.

"My god," she said, "he'll shoot the damned dog just to get at me."

Using Pendleton, Tom would carve out her center and lay it like a peeled banana in the sun until she blended into the ground and would be something he'd scrape from his shoes before he got in the car.

No rational thing Jared said could stop her leaving.

She pulled into her clothes, and cussed through the speedy drive, past Goodwill, up her own hilltop she bought with the money from the split with Neal, fearing Pendleton's belly hugged a bullet. Tom would have maybe planted two there to seal the case.

Pendleton padded across the porch with his dry dish in his mouth, dragging it so it scraped the boards. Christ, she forgot to water the dog. That's how loose at the ends Tom had her.

She petted and crooned, "Aw, c'mere, Pen, pretty Pen, my beauty-boy, Pen, my love." She let her heart calm and thought on what Jared said when she left, "Everything doesn't have anger at the source."

Bending down to kiss Pendleton, she'd swear she heard a waterfall, though no stream crossed her land. Maybe Tom had turned on the faucet in the kitchen. No, her Bonneville showed off its tilted, lonely park job in the driveway; Tom wasn't even here. Was it thunder then? She leaned into Pendleton, listening to the air while sun hazed up the sky. It took shutting out her own heartbeat to identify the bees – simple, foraging bees, tuning up a dead log, doing what-next for survival, abandoning the once-sweet hive, manufacturing their new home from what their bodies made.

The Upper Hand

"Pauline's a woman can't be satisfied," said his inner voice, but Jared aimed to try. His would topple all the other rickety-built love she'd known. In rubbing his forearm he smoothed down the caution prickling there. He could feel more pluck than luck funneling into this pursuit, and that was mighty okay. He'd run ahead blinded by his own devices before, hoping the woman would teach him lessons worth learning. Knowledge was acquired; just say that. Where every woman whittled, shaped him a little more to the form Pauline wanted without her even knowing her own wanting.

He would show her she was changing him, he would prove it; he was on the road to demonstration.

Flying west in the Pontiac across Kansas, he'd crossed two states and his priors made him legal wandering nowhere but Euphoria, Illinois.

If his brother had not been lost in Afghanistan, Sten would have said, "Shit, when did you ever tuck your tail to rules?"

It might play out badly, but before the bad there would be play, the rolling dice and the coming up short. If Jared drove fast and far enough and put maximum miles between them, he might knot Pauline up with him for good. Or he could be axing his future.

His plan: go away and make her come back to him, choose him. Make her come back of her own accord, her taking the leap. Jared would tell you, the heart hidden is the heart that's wanted. Or the old cliché about how distance conquers lovers. Distance was cement, it was super glue, and he intended slathering a ton along I-70, where he knew, he just sensed, Pauline would track him.

"You got to go away to get it," Sten always said. "Pretend disinterest. It ain't an outright lie. It's weave and duck, it's strategy. The girl always comes around."

Sten knew his birds and guns and shit, but his women advice hit short, or had in the past.

Jared felt his brother's instincts deserved a second chance. Hence this flight.

His offenses had not been so criminal – only in the eyes of the state. The state, which would be hauling his ass back to Euphoria to stand handcuffed before the bench again.

"The law fucks with your life," he yelled into the wind wailing through open windows at eighty-five miles an hour. Alone as far as the eye could see, he kicked it to ninety.

Hence the monotonous blur of agriculture, and a highway that encouraged visions. Flat land raised up and waved at him, it buckled under the weighty horizon. A storm ahead shoved columns of rain for Jared to penetrate. He blinked his itchy eyes and drove straight into the deluge.

If rain ruled forty days and nights, who would he bring with him to help repopulate the world? In a word – Pauline, Pauline, Pauline. He knew his ruling obsessions:

when he wanted a woman he wanted her bad, he wanted her through and through, bad through, very very bad. Never wanted a woman as thoroughly and badly as he wanted Pauline. Of course, he said that about every woman he'd ever loved, all the way back to his high school crush, Debra. Seemed his mistake lay in letting her know how crazy she made him. One night after coming off third shift at Providence South, he told her about an unconscious girl whose condition would not vacate his mind.

"Working the air intake, it was right next to her, connected to the ventilator. Car accident, somebody said. God, I don't want that to ever happen to you, Debra. You've got to start following rules."

"Listen to you, Jared," she said, "going on about rules."

He grabbed her shoulders and shook her a little. "Swear to me you'll buckle in from now on."

"I'll do what I want." Debra wiggled from his grasp, and high-pitch giggled. "And what I want right now is ..." She unzipped his jeans, which was the principal distraction and reward in loving her. The way she made him feel so good, he forgot disasters on deserted roads and hospital hauntings. He was obsessed with her for all the wrong reasons; she was his means of forgetting.

During that summer when her cousin, Marnie, came to visit, Providence held their annual picnic.

"We can't go and not take Marnie," Deb said. "You got two arms."

Marnie had been in town three days in which, already, Debra had molded to her like a twin. Debra said they slept in the same bed. What eighteen-year-old boy would not be rocked by that? The cousins giggled and squealed and leaped in their high-heeled sandals as they moved across the parking lot, their arms linking Jared three-way in the middle. His feet barely touched the asphalt, borne along as he was by them. They were taking him to his own picnic, like a prized entry in a pie contest, like a piglet they'd raised.

"Double date, eh?" Mike Garsman declared when Jared introduced the girls. Mike, his supervisor from Maintenance, stood grilling burgers and dogs, wincing against the smoke and the sizzle. A grease-soiled chef's apron barely wrapped his gut. Jared especially sheltered Debra, to make clear the boundaries. He didn't care if the guy moved in on Marnie.

At the picnic, he saw Debra and Mike with their heads together over beers. Employee picnics, where the beer flowed freely, extended from hot afternoon into dark muggy night. Everybody got a buzz, got sleepy, then went about acquiring that second buzz. Who knows how much they'd sucked down total? Jared wandered, not for the first time, off to the woods to piss. He might have taken the long way back, or got lost looking at ferns or the latticework in the trees upward with the moon behind. Either way, he approached Mike and Deb and she was scowling and pointing her beer bottle, the way Jared knew she'd use a prop to make her point. She'd pointed a few things out to him, his faults mostly.

Such judgments floated through his soppy brain while he crunched moss and chickweed and mole tunnels underfoot. Mike had a flat dirty way of talking, so Jared imagined he'd laid on Debra one too many sleazy jokes and she was rising at him in righteous indignation. Her sweetness canceled out her sour. He didn't think about where was Marnie. He forgot Marnie completely, wrenched Debra away from Mike so fast she dropped the bottle and it smashed at their feet.

In the car, he grilled her. "What did he say to you?"

"I don't know. Where were you?"

"What did he say, Deb?"

"I don't know ... something smutty."

"Like what?"

"I don't know." Her voice went high and shrill. "Down in the garden, what did I do down in the garden."

"What? What garden?"

She fell into the crying he knew was coming, and in between sobbing she said, "I wanted you there. I wanted you where I was, that's all. Where were you?"

Where was he? Where had he been? Jared was driving, he was steering the car right then and he shouldn't have been behind any wheel. And still they cruised on. Sanity cruised on past; the regret, the fear, the logic all cruised on ahead of his head.

He said, "In the woods, taking a leak." And then he remembered, like it was a dream, jerking off to a vision of Marnie under the trees. Imagining Marnie stripped and stippled by moonlight in front of him, too far away to touch and so he touched himself. But Marnie had never really been there.

Why didn't his body speak to hers anymore? He wanted to say this to Debra. They sat in the driveway of her parents' house. He bent to kiss her and she let him get closer than close, then ducked away. Bitch, always trying to prove she was in charge. So if she ducked, he would duck too, and he did.

They both tucked into themselves. Debra exploded out of the car and ran into the house.

Marnie said, "Whoa. Shit." She'd been in the back seat the whole time, like contraband.

"Sorry we didn't stay for the fireworks," Jared said.

She shrugged and he could smell her all woodsy and the fruit scent of her hair. "I'm not that wild about fireworks anyway. It was just something to do. Got a light?" she said, angling with a cigarette from behind.

They went to the backyard to smoke.

"Attentive – maybe it's one of my faults," he told Marnie. "But I knew Mike pissed off Deb. I wanted to get to the source of it, to deck Mike if I needed to, but more to soothe Debra. To show her that guy's mouth dredged the bottom and wasn't nothing he said could be of any light or brightness or meaning for her to hold onto."

"You're bugging the shit out of her, hounding her. The girl likes her secrets."

"I'm trying to love her."

"You're trying too hard."

"I'm not trying at all."

"Exactly. It's just the way you are." Marnie sighed, like Jared was too hard for any girl to take. They sat on the topmost level of the picnic table, their feet resting on the bench for sitting, leaning forward, elbows on knees, all confident and careless, with Debra slammed inside for the night.

Marnie took his hand. "Deb needs to blow off some steam," she said. "Just leave her alone. Tomorrow will be a different story. Meantime, why don't you 'not try at all' with me?"

Sten's words about going off and returning, they seemed to apply, as did Marnie's hand down the back of Jared's jeans in the good dark. She smelled citrusy. Jared thought of fish, how fish needs some lemon to cut its fishy smell and taste. He felt himself a water creature; they were way in the ocean deep, the world over their heads no consequence.

"Ain't that how love is?" he said into her open mouth. "How it sweeps over you, causing nothing but waves you gotta ride?"

"Mmmhmm." She hummed-kissed him, wrapping his tongue with hers, bait. The whole world was squirming, desirous. And he knew that woods scene earlier had been no drunk dream.

Or this here now was dream. Either way, he wasn't opening his eyes.

"A hummingbird is just a great big bee, a greater buzz," she said.

Jared said, "I'll show you buzz."

After Marnie left, he told Debra he regretted it thoroughly. That he thoroughly thoroughly loved her, loved her dearly, loved her madly badly, very very badly. She was the one, THE one. If she couldn't see that then she didn't see anything.

"Honey, listen to me," he said. "My heart falling to yours. I will always be falling in your direction."

Sten had been wrong about how you could go away from love and the love comes back stronger. Such bullshit.

"I didn't say screw her cousin," Sten said.

The girls might have been in cahoots. He took Sten's advice, twisted it and cast it in the ocean. He was casting and he was what had been cast. He'd fucked up.

Alone in the apartment, when he knelt and his bones on the beat-up, uncovered wood ached as much as his insides, he threw himself around at the end of a mad fisherman's line. Trying to catch some break, some fish, some ease from the hurt. He swallowed every pill in the place and smoked whatever Sten had left behind. He knocked over furniture and appliances, his hands clutching at the ends of someone's ravaged arms.

It was day and it was night and then it was day again. His mouth was where the fisherman's hook had landed – foul-tasting and barbed. He managed to find the sink, to drink, to let water gush across his face and into his scalp. He felt it beading there, crawling through, the mice and the mites all in the roots. He used up the rest of the day cutting his long hair and shaving his head. It's a wonder he didn't slit his throat. Or cut off an ear. And misquoting Sir Thomas Wyatt – who even read, much less quoted, the Elizabethans? – he muttered, "There heart, how like you this?"

Bald-headed, feeling mole-like and newly emerged, he grabbed what lay nearest, his jacket, slashed it with his knife. "How like you this? And this? And this?" His breath absorbed by the effort. The apartment spun around him.

Marnie and Debra merged into one she-devil woman, a goddess-conniver, when he thought back on it, a memory now more than ten years old, the first love that breaks a guy, digs him deep, toughens him up.

He cuts his teeth on her, right? Or she cuts hers on him, leaving a fissure whose edges may, with the right bravado and enough time, close over but never disappear. Harbored pain was what it was. Plenty of women since, but come the right one at the right time with her particular elbow into Jared's solar plexus and he'd be laid wide open.

"All your innards for the taking of her slap-happy beak," Sten would say.

Beaks, like the cartoons Heckle and Jeckle on the Saturday morning show they both, as boys, laughed over and imitated like little magpies. Their mom used to say, "Smart-alecky birds, I'd like to slap-happy them, slap them silly some's what I'd do."

With cartoon magpies unreachable, Sten and Jared were stand-ins. Mom's lickings turned them more smartass than any damned birds on a wire. That was in Pittsburgh, where they flew the coop, in the city on a river, industrial, mucky, and un-fucking-lucky. After Sten graduated vocational, he scored a welding job, got an apartment, sheltered Jared there. They got out from under, yes, they did.

"Don't let anybody tell you it can't be done," Sten said, "flipping a bad situation on its goddamned ear. You can do it yourself if you have to."

And then Sten enlisted, joined the army, turned all governmental and patriotic, so's Jared had to swallow cold beer just to quell his vomit. Once his brother left, Jared drove west without stopping. First night brought him to Evansville – new city, familiar river. Landscape and weather so akin to Pittsburgh it nearly pushed him back to the highway, but he stayed two nights, three, four, and on into weeks, enrolled in community college to learn heating and air conditioning. Mom always said, above all, people need their heat. Even the two-year degree programs offered electives.

He'd loved king and queen stories when he was a boy, knights and their jousting, so he signed up for Elizabethan Poetry, and you might have thought: what a mistake. But no, it slayed him. It torqued his heart and blew his mind. He suffered a breakdown.

Sten wrote en route to Pakistan, "You were a time bomb waiting to go off, bro. Don't think it's your fault coz that pin was pulled long time ago." The email arrived three weeks after Jared got out of what he jokingly called "the mental ward."

Two weeks later, Sten's communiques quit.

All of this transpired on one side of the Wabash. Then Jared crossed the bridge into Illinois, coasting into Euphoria, the whole trip in his brother's Pontiac a sort of tribute to Sten, as he'd not be back to reclaim it.

Coming out of the rain, out of God's Colorado car wash, Jared saw pink, he saw lemon, he saw indigo in the sky.

He'd seen the way Pauline eyed his coat. She stroked his arm as if the suede were a pelt.

Yes, she'd petted him. She set her fingers on the scars he'd sewn up. He fell for her the first minute he saw her at the Goodwill. And yes, he'd maneuvered to anchor the end of that sidewalk he knew she made part of her route. Don't call him stalker.

"Call me attentive," he said to Pauline.

She raised her eyebrows to him where they stood paused at the edge of the gully, and said nothing, but he could tell she was assembling it all in her pretty little mind. She was building him before his very eyes, building him new.

He'd been torn, limping, ragged and piecemeal for so long, hunchback from a horror movie, hugging his broken parts, his heart tucked deep, an innermost plum pit. Like the rings of a tree trunk or the levels of the earth from crust down to magma, Jared carried his scars from the time of Debra and Saturday cartoons and Sten stepping in the way of Mom's half-ass smacks, when the two of them took whatever she doled out because they preferred her furor over her lassitude.

No son of Euphoria, son of nobody in the bleak Midwest.

But he belonged to Pauline, who built him into a better man than he'd ever been. And Pauline belonged to Tom. Somebody always belonged to somebody else. Even Debra belonged to Marnie more than she had to Jared.

As excuse for not leaving her husband, at least not yet, Pauline said, "If someone's dangerous it doesn't matter that you let them say a few lines while you hold onto the lap of your skirt. Your skirt, like your tongue, is just something else to hold."

Jared had seen and met Tom; Tom wasn't dangerous. Tom was a self-centered lout. Love was about having the upper hand. Jared thought of his mom's hard slap aiming down, and poorboy-him froze to the spot, cognizant of approaching pain and no will to get from under before it hit. Yeah, the fucking upper hand. It had him.

Tense

Pauline cranked open her granny's old ironing board, filled the Procter Silex from Goodwill with water, and clicked the iron to the steam setting. In the back of the house, Tom screeched dresser drawers off-kilter and cursed. Beyond his mumbling, Pauline tried expanding her senses to embrace Jared across the miles that he, this minute, was logging between them.

He'd ordered her out of his Chevy from her backseat stowaway, and she vacated, mopey-faced, beside the car, hoping for a reversal. Tom had arrived home two days early. Unexpected didn't approach the half of it.

Jared left her with, "Pauline, you need to be present."

After she heard "present" she thought "gift," and Jared was her unexpected gift in the lost and lonely time Led Zeppelin sang of. He might be gone, but they would never be done. She'd elbow him if she had to, to gain a little ground. Love was a competition that way, one or the other proving beyond measure that troth would be made. The old word for promise seemed right, as troth was the very pith of love, its white and sticky essence, the DNA, single central cell, the future fixation.

She'd gone ahead and dared, when she said, "This time come home with me," to Jared, and set the stage for a showdown on her own turf, a house which had witnessed slithery remarks and seething but no punches thrown. So civil and sarcastic, her life with Tom. The bite without the teeth. She'd tried biting back and all it got her was lonely.

Pauline stretched her chin to the ceiling then bent her neck to her chest to shake the knots from ironing. She would not lie naked soaking in the tub while Tom wandered past, his gaze either perturbed or appreciative, each skip in and out like steps in his planned robbery of her, while somewhere a timer ticked on a stack of dynamite.

He ambushed her in the kitchen as she took down the ironing board. She held the folded contraption in front of her to buffer words that must have been avalanching in him since he'd run Jared from the house earlier.

"I'm killing myself just keeping an eye on you, Pauline."

"Who said you had to? Who said you should?"

"Marriage vows, babe. The preacher. City Hall, government, God."

"As if you cared about any one of them."

"I'm law-abiding. And I'm sensible. Can you call me otherwise?"

She raised her eyebrow.

"Tell me what's what. That's all I ask." He was always jutting his chin in a defiance that sexied him up. Pauline could not explain why this failed to sway her.

"Because at last you've been known," Jared had told her.

"You don't know me," she said to Tom, hugging the ironing board. The metal felt good piercing her armpits.

"What's that mean?"

"You talk like you're interested, but it's only talk."

Tom's turn for the quizzical eyebrow. He pointed at her, he pointed at himself. "What else you want? What do you think you're missing?"

"Where you hear what I say before I even open my mouth."

Tom looked at her like she was cracked, like she should be committed and watched over in a place where his dad and stepmom had been assigned, where medical personnel would tie you down if they had to.

"Fairytale, Pauline. That's what you're waiting on."

She shrugged. "Probably." Then she went to hide the ironing board in the hallway closet with the vacuum cleaner and the dust mop and the pole for snagging high up corner cobwebs.

She felt herself a tenuous filament that got spun out of neglect and lack of friction.

He tagged behind her. "What important secrets are you afraid to tell? Tell me what I need to know *to know you.*"

"I can't say, Tom."

"You can't, or won't?"

"What makes you even care now?"

His face took on the kindest, most sober look. "I'm your husband, babe. Why wouldn't I care?"

That clanged an alarm inside her. Perhaps she'd been interpreting the signs wrong. He loved her as much as ever but forgot to show it. Life for everybody leveled into routine, but beyond such low expectations, Pauline craved. She craved.

Not *every*body is you, Pauline, she knew Jared would say. She hung onto that. Pauline was between a rock and the hard ground because both her men loved her. She was their flint against the stone, and they both wanted to burn.

She called Tom her King of Disorder. Telltale Tom, with the clues of his presence: flipped container lids, kicked free sheets, counter ketchup splatters. The walls of the microwave held his small detonations. The large miseries he spilled Pauline's way. He came and went as he pleased. His truck driving gigs easily covered whatever he wished hidden.

She was no snooping wife, but frequency and inattention and the times his cell was unavailable? Come *on*. Could be she didn't care that much, that she never should have married him. Jared embodied her realization of that.

She once joked to Jared that she took it on the chin from Tom, and then she had to collar him from vaulting out of bed and zooming across town to pound her husband.

"I mean I accept his oddities. He's never hit me."

Jared halted his half-dressed rushing. "And he never will."

She grabbed his open belt to drag him back to bed. She felt she owed him a piece of what she normally kept to herself. "Tom raises his voice. But violence isn't in him."

Jared said, "You wouldn't lie to me?"

As he brought her to his bare chest, she heard his heart roaring like a locomotive, like a tireless ocean where she was his tiny boat.

Pauline suspected Jared would take abuse, unfazed, until you tripped his line, that one unspecified line of his, and then he'd leap into a darkness not even he knew the way out of. She wondered if she'd pushed him to that point. She wished he'd drag her into that darkness, too, where he might carry a weapon. Not the gun thrilling her, but that he'd tote one with the idea of claiming her against any and all else. She wiped with a yellow sponge at the mess Tom had made when slapping together his sandwich.

From the window she spied Tom's sister, Fiona, walking up the gravel. Plenty old enough to have her own car and to drive, Fee fussed with neither.

Pauline stepped out and called from the porch, "He's not here," and, "Didn't walk all the way here, did you, Fee?"

"Cab," Fiona said, striving for breath. The girl carried extra weight on her hips and across her middle, but was still young enough that it was a selling point.

Fiona's face flushed from the uphill trek. "Driver's waiting down below. I was a little short on the fare."

"As if that's my problem," Pauline said, but with Fiona present, she matured. She dashed inside for her wallet. They had both loved rocker-man Neal and had both been ditched by him, and – oh, how the world gets its laughs – had been kin for twenty-two months. Fiona inspired competition.

Pauline crashed down the porch just as Fee set her first step up in impossibly high-heeled sandals. "Somebody's got to pay," Pauline yelled, skittering down the gravel, leaping from the house and echoes of Tom's accusations and Fiona with her multi-colored patchwork bag, big enough to carry a toaster oven. Maybe Jared idled at the driveway's end, shooting the shit with the cabbie. Maybe he'd U-turned it back to her.

What few thunderstorms shook Euphoria this third dry summer sent the rocks running down Pauline's hill, left bald patches and ruts that would jar the best suspension. No wonder the cab refused to drive Fiona to the door.

The Checker idled in the empty road. A tan, muscled arm stretched out the open window, awaiting bills on her palm. The cabbie was a she. No other car in sight.

Pauline gazed down at the trail left by the taxi's exit as Pendleton came loping toward her out of the roadside brush.

"Baby," Pauline crooned, offering her fingers to his tongue. She bent to her gorgeous, all-forgiving, ever-loving dog. "You're so good to me." She put her face in his neck fur, inhaling his deep animal smell, the earth, the weeds he'd been tearing through to get to her. "Always good," she said. "Always here."

The dog watched when she pulled back, clear-eyed, as Jared would, almost focusing past her, as if seeing ahead and trying to influence future-Pauline's metabolic makeup.

Jared had told her, "In me is an intensity for you I've never known, Pauline. You're my virus, and you're multiplying inside me, toppling me."

"Oh yeah, I'm your fever," she joked.

"You are," he insisted, his hands gripping the tops of her arms, his voice devoid of emotion. He claimed he'd have no joking about it.

"You can't dream away the rough stuff," Jared had told her. "Some things only you can act on, but I'll be here for you, Pauline, in whatever way you need."

"Huh," she said, scratching Pendleton's ears. "Big promises. Look where he is?"

Pendleton's ears perked alert.

"A state or two away, flying his own road, dazzled by the California light. Law's going to get him, Pen," she whispered. "And then what will we do?"

She walked up the hill, wishing that locking Jared in her mind's eye would cloak him from anyone out to do him harm. Pendleton ran off, and she heard him warbling the distinctive croak that signaled he'd found what he wouldn't give up on.

Fiona, snapping her chewing gum, withdrew her cell phone from her mammoth purse and set it on the kitchen table while Pauline poured two glasses of iced tea.

"He's got a gun, you know." Pauline tried sounding flip and unconcerned.

Fiona blew a bubble until it popped. "Tom doesn't need a gun," she said, sucking gum back into her mouth.

"No?" Pauline said.

"He can hit like a truck."

In two years Pauline had never seen Tom fight. Even when he had a choke hold on Jared, he let her lover go. Considering Fiona's remark, Tom's restraint made her feel peculiar. Pauline opened the fridge and hid behind the door. "I don't speak for Tom, what he needs or doesn't need." She took a cantaloupe from the crisper drawer, opened a sheet of newspaper, and commenced gutting the melon.

"'Course not. Why should you?" Fiona said. She kept touching her phone, clicking it open and checking for missed calls, texts, whatever. It crazied Pauline.

"Can't you just be present?" she said, then went on, "Why should only movie stars live movie stars lives?" She tasted a piece of fruit off the knife's edge.

"That's dangerous," Fiona said, with raised eyebrows, one of them pierced.

Pauline directed her knife. "I'm disappointed in this." She hadn't discovered the secret to selecting fruit. She wrapped up the rinds and the seeds and put the mess in the garbage.

"Can I taste some?" Fiona said.

"You like this kind of melon?"

"I might. I don't know. Let me try."

Fiona speared a piece with the fork Pauline handed her and then Fiona ate the cantaloupe until it was gone. Pauline didn't have an appetite anyway. They didn't talk of Tom or Neal or men, and they sure didn't talk of Jared.

"Tom's promises never change," Pauline said. "Blah blah blah." Fiona looked at Pauline, and Pauline looked back.

Pauline whispered, "Am I cockeyed? Have I got it all wrong?"

"You think I know my brother, but nobody knows Tom."

"I like to believe I got a bead on him; we're married after all."

Fiona gave her the sly eye she'd no doubt employed when stealing Neal away from Pauline. "Marriage gives you a better perspective?"

Bitchy Little Sister observed Tom and Pauline when they were knobby-kneed twelve-year-olds, bike-riding friends and nothing more. Fiona, in the doorway with her Barbies, or her ponies – anything with long hair for brushing – stood spookily quiet, almost part of the décor. You could feel her yearning to run with them, but she didn't. Though she had no problem shutting down her reticence once she left home at sixteen and fell in with Neal Bone's Band, specifically with Neal. She slapped Pauline with their shared memory at every opportunity.

"You knew Neal like I knew Neal, right?" Fiona said.

Pauline nodded, blank. She expected this not to hurt anymore and was amazed when it still did.

"Well, blah blah blah," Fiona said.

The world pierced then removed its needle, one small biopsy to excise Neal. Tom was like chemo follow up, both poison and cure. Pauline sometimes had this thought about herself: she was a sorry-ass survivor and there wasn't enough left in her to give Jared.

Fiona flipped open her cell. "I should get out of here."

Pauline dropped her sister-in-law at the Dusty Rider Lounge, then rolled on through the next intersection in her big boat of a car. In review, she could not pin down the why of Fiona's visit. Town lured her, kept her from the house where everything sat too still, the empty Tupperware bowl, and all the knives wiped clean and stacked in the drawer.

On the street she drove past a boy with a lime-green cast from his wrist to his elbow. He piqued her interest, with all that screaming color, and she followed him at a decent distance to the hospital. She parked and entered through Emergency's automated doors, took in what the room offered: insomniac, man on crutches, the unsettled, the spent. The boy with the cast sat, leaning into a beleaguered woman Pauline guessed was his mother from the way he curled in and she gave him shelter. The woman's eyes met Pauline's, and those eyes alone rendered the mother beautiful, no longer worn, but used up in one purpose— loving her boy. This woman made Pauline feel vacant in her childlessness and at the same time limitless in what she, herself, was able to give. A check for the hospital's new lab? Volunteerism? Should she try to donate blood?

Two women together waited in the molded orange chairs bolted to the floor. No junkies in their high states would be coming in and lifting one of these babies through the plate glass. The women were older, a grandmother's and a mother's age. Sincere and oblivious in their bathrobes, they appeared light years ahead of Pauline in know-how and experience. She heard the younger say to the older, "I'm trying to get well." And the grandma nodded, closing her watery eyes.

Pauline tried out the daughter's line. She whispered, "I'm trying to get well." She felt the flutter in her chest, as if medics had put their paddles to her. Along a westbound highway, with no destination except "go," a man drove too fast and without enough thought to her when he had her heart right there in his glove box, the thief. She intended to find him and jolt him the way she'd just been jolted, to clear his eyes of what distracted him and make him see her – see selfish, scatter-brained, steadfast her.

Crease

"Considerable grief" is what teachers wrote more than a few times on the comments side of Jared's grade school reports. His mother repeated it when reading the teachers' words, pinning him to the wall with this not-so-brand-new news. Sten accused him of considerable grief when they crashed among the field stubble, looking for the dove he'd shot out of the sky, which they never did locate.

Considerable grief Jared had brought to Pauline, with Tom's knowledge and judgment on them, so he lit out, resisting blame for the way the world hammered him and those he loved.

It's probably time to admit what he did back when. There was trouble with that knife he pulled on a jerk in a DairyMart pestering a girl in line, a girl too young, who sidled up to the lanky-hair with tattoos from his wrists to his shoulders. She dangled a ten under the inked guy's nose and said, "Buy me cigarettes?"

Jared watched the scum look her through, his lust burning away her few fresh clothes.

Her overbite was the kind of off-kilter men loved, especially on young things.

"You can keep what's left," she said, pressing the bill on him.

His mouthful of jumbled teeth sneered. "What's left? Sweetie, I'm in for the whole kit and kaboodle." He palmed the ten and reached for her ass with the moneyed hand. She recoiled, backing into Jared.

"Whoops." She giggled.

Jared's smile bent tolerant and telepathic in an effort to show her how to show calm, but she was taking no notice. The guy with her ten wiped the bearded part of his face, beamed interest that might not scare you if you ignored the dentistry. They three awaited the cashier guy refunding lottery tickets for a woman who stared at them, and with a tug on her shirt hem concealed a strip of waist-level fat.

In contrast, the teenage girl had a package tucked tight in her bicycle pants and cut-off tee.

She flaunted her little chest and got caught in her flaunting, working it, never meaning to deliver. She maybe thought herself a fish who'd escape the slimy net. Girls pegged themselves safe in their giggly tier of bubble gum and fruit-smelling hair until the first time they got yanked good by that ponytail and pushed to their knees by a scumbag. Then they learn the lesson.

Lottery Lady moved on out the tinkle-rigged door.

Tattoo Guy hefted his six-pack on the counter, snapped fried pork rinds from the snack clip, and reached for his chain wallet. "Pack of Camels, no filter, and ..." he turned to check with the girl and encountered Jared. She cowered at the line's end, berry smells lifting from her nape. Surely everyone in the DairyMart caught the aroma of fruit, and the thread of violence growing skinny.

The girl pressed her hand in the center of Jared's back. "Salems," she whispered.

"Salems," Jared said.

"And a pack of Salems," said the spidery-armed guy, showing off his malformed teeth. He paid and pocketed the change, tossed the pack of menthols at the girl – surprised her, but she caught them.

Tattoo Guy said, "Lookin' ahead to our exchange outside, sweetie."

Jared said, "Respect, man. Just cool it."

Tattoo Guy's watery blues had pinprick, soulless centers. Appealing to reason or respect wouldn't cut it. Both the girl and the hopped-up jerk were strangers to Jared, and he should have learned from previous times when he'd painted himself in as the rescuer.

In the DairyMart, rage and miscue heated the knife weighing down his pocket, the blade aching for his hand.

"Just what I'm due, buddy. Got the little lady her cigs, didn't I?"

Cigs – also why Jared had stepped in.

"She don't owe you. She paid. She overpaid."

Tattoo Guy returned his bag to the counter with a reconsidered slowness. "That so?" the prick said. His beltless jeans bore weeks' worth of grime. One of the pockets might have concealed a wrench.

In knife versus wrench, blade wins, Sten always said.

Pauline insisted, "You fight, you better fight fair," but Jared didn't know Pauline then.

Showing the fucker the blade conjured her, in that Jared's life sequenced straight to Pauline from there, initiated the minute the Nervous Nellie cashier hit the under-the-counter panic button.

Tattoo Guy measured his knife against Jared's and said, "Don't give me no grief, son."

The girl squealed and skittered to the side cooler

holding the ten-pound ice bags.

"Ea-sy," the man behind the counter drawled. He supposed help was on the way and could afford to stick in his two cents of Mr. Calm. He was the overalls type, the tobacco-chaw type, though he right then sported neither of these accents. His slicked-back hair drooped, he perspired, and his shirt rode up the back of his Wranglers.

"This ain't no holdup. Relax," Tattoo Guy said. He waved the knifepoint. "This is just between me and Buster here."

The counter man said, "You want to take it outside?"

If other shoppers lurked, they stuck to the rear aisles, worried about bullets.

Jared held his knife steady and thoroughly on display, different from the *en garde* stance with long sharpened sticks he played at with Sten in the woods when they were boys. This was serious weaponry drawn in a convenience store in front of witnesses and with no backing down.

"Leave the girl alone. You just leave. And there'll be nothing more."

"Oh, sure, Sonny, and color me a yellow stripe down my back while you're at it. Hell, no. After you and me settle, that honey's got some sweet for me, don't ya, sugar?" The sleaze made eyes at the girl by the ice chest and she and her shoulders curled into the big fabric bag she slung there.

A girl like that could hide in her purse, tiny her and big old fringey thing.

Tattoo Guy pointed to the girl with his knife. "Probably's got half a wardrobe in there. Never know when she might not make it home a night."

"Why don't you take your cracklins and your piss-beer and move on out of here?" Jared said. His hand itched. This guy looked as good a target as any. Just like the dummies he and Sten had practiced on, bodies made from corn husks of a thousand spent summer rows. Nothing but dry insides calling for pointy. Jared even thought he heard the stalks rustling but that was the DairyMart air conditioner rattling up in the wall by where the lottery ticket wheels were mounted.

Jared shook his head against the rat-tat-tat, against the psycho with the drawn knife and eyes a-gleaming. "Head on out, why don't you?"

"And miss the show you're promising'? Not on your life, sonny."

Jared knew he shouldn't have let this lowlife see he could get to him with name calling.

So much you should keep stowed inside the vest, Sten advised. So much grief I'd rather not hear, his mom sighed, squinty-eyed, in one of her many stewed afternoons. Inside the DairyMart, day shifted a shade toward dusk. The dust motes strangled in their suspension. The world and every particle of air lived, funneling into the DairyMart where collision happened, was meant to happen.

Jared brought the man's lip to his knife. He placed the blade there and the crazy's red lines reddened further the milk around his fierce blue eyes, the bloodshot shot through with greater blood. "Get. Out. Go," Jared said.

The girl shrieked, and Jared turned his head her way.

Why his opponent didn't stick Jared good up under the ribs then the way Jared himself had been taught, we'll never know. The creep instead slashed back and forth atop Jared's bare arms. Flesh wounds, showy. Things healed; he had a body that proved that.

Blood on the counter, on the DairyMart pitted linoleum, on their boots, both their boots, two pair, four shoes, and the girl wailing, "Oh, my God, you're killing him, stop."

Announced by a bell, the law strode in.

"Problem here, Satchel?"

Counter Guy lifted his hand, all nonchalant response now that backup had arrived. The girl emerged from her purse and stood so her small breasts perked the front of her shirt once more. "They're fighting," she screeched. "Can't you see?"

Jared palmed his knife into hiding.

The Tattoo Creep licked blood from his lip. "Over you, gal," he said.

The deputy observed them with a hard-ass, impassive expression. Every crease was creased in the fabric he wore and in his forehead; his buttons and badges and name tag glinted. His hat set level with the horizon.

"You boys making a mess, aren't ya? Just look at this floor. Satchel, you got a towel behind there for this one?"

The girl said, "Aren't you going to tell them to drop their weapons?"

"Honey," the lawman said, "this ain't TV." Then he kicked Tattoo Guy behind the knees and the son of a bitch crumpled to the floor. His knife flew under the freezer case. The guy stayed down there coughing.

"Disarmed," the deputy confirmed to the girl. He smiled at Jared. "Now I'll have yours. You handing it over nice and slow will eliminate me taking it from you in such a fashion as you've just witnessed from your friend."

"Friend, not hardly," Jared said. He slowly opened his hand and the cuss's squeaky-scrubbed fingers plucked the knife.

"Yes, well, we figured that, didn't we? Or there'd not be so much red messing up Satchel's fine establishment, eh? Got a mop back there and stock boy to wield it?"

"Nah. Just me," Satchel said. "I'll do it once you run them out."

"You need to make a statement, honey," the lawman said to the girl. "Witnessing and all."

She started her shrinking routine again.

"Witness?" Tattoo Guy spit, lifting his face from the floor. "She's the all-over cause."

The deputy leaned his knee into the guy's back and cuffed him. "What do these pictures here mean anyway?"

"I got my rights. I won't say. I want a lawyer. My tats, they don't require no explaining to you."

The deputy kneed him further until the guy's nose touched the floor. "Just making conversation." Tattoo Guy curled like a shrimp there, silent, might as well be underwater.

Satchel said, "How the mighty have fallen." Then he eyed Jared. "What about this one? He was first to pull the knife."

"He was helping," the girl piped up. She'd ripped the outsides of the Salems, had packed the cigarettes against the heel of her hand and tapped one out. She could have been Bette Davis looking for a light, all her sashay now on display, the bad guys nabbed.

"Don't drop that wad of trash, ma'am, or I'll have you in for littering," the deputy said. He brought Tattoo Guy, not kindly, up from the floor, started shoving him to the door. Satchel skirted his counter and made the bells ring, ever the helpful aide. "You're next," the lawman said to Jared.

In walked his partner. Jared could see the deputy had preferred kinging it over everybody and the situation. His hands, rivered with blood, half curled open at the end of his loose, bloodied arms. He felt chicken all of a sudden, and light-headed, he felt like goddamned flapping his wings. He almost squawked, but he bit his tongue.

The junior partner said, "We got to get this one sewn up."

"Don't hurt him," the girl said. She'd located her lighter in the bottom mess of that big bag of hers and now puffed one of the menthols that had ignited the trouble.

Junior said, "We're not hurting, we're here to help, ma'am."

He cuffed Jared's hands forward in consideration of his bleeding.

Arms wrapped in Satchel's ratty towels like a half-mummy, Jared rode in the back of the squad car with the jerk who'd cut him. And even though the armrest dug his side, and with his face twisted away so his neck ached, he smelled the Tattoo Guy's gross weight and breadth and hate.

To where they were bound seemed an incredible, dreamlike distance. The girl chattered beside the king-deputy in the front seat while the junior lawman remained at the DairyMart to record Satchel's statement. Stories featuring Jared at the incipient center of a knife fight rattlerang inside "that Tower of Babel" his mother used to call his never-stop-jabbering mind.

If he didn't have to press towels to his wounded arms he would have instead held his head in his hands and squeezed.

As he never actually attacked the scumbag with the knife, Jared pled guilty to assault.

The judge ruled "Stay in the county, report periodically to probation, and perform community service."

The court, or the system, lined him up with Goodwill to

man their unloading zone. Nothing demanding about people driving up with their life's discards and Jared helping cart it away. He showed up as part of his plea, mostly tilting back Dr. Peppers he brought with his lunch in a Coleman cooler to the sorting dock, more an apron of broke-up blacktop where the dryer vented outside.

He didn't and couldn't and cared not to remember Tattoo Guy's punishment.

Only a few days into his restitution when Jared sighted a woman in slim jeans, sensible button shirt and Frye boots step to Goodwill's front, then he peeked around the building's side after she vanished. He followed her, at a respectful pace, through the store. That was the first of many times he tailed Pauline down the flannel shirt aisle, hung back when she paused at the jewelry case of grandmothers' rhinestones and god-awful fake gold.

"I'm wary of falsity," she said, looking down through the display glass.

Jared drew close. What else could a man do if he wanted not to miss her single word?

"Not my intent," he said.

"Oh, you have an intent, do you?" She tapped her fingernail to indicate the salesgirl should open the lock. "I'd like to see that," she said.

Her meanings, he discovered, always fell two ways, and he liked this coy style of Pauline's. And she was damned hot, her ass made for those jeans, her boot heels synchronizing their heights so he confronted the undiluted hazel in her eyes, which she widened once she knew she had his attention. "Pearls are timeless, don't you think?"

Captivated, he nodded.

Pivoting to the counter, she said, "Show me those, there, that choker."

Pearls, which she modeled for him as she stretched her lovely throat. Pearls, which he bought for her after she laughingly told the girl, "Better put them back before my willpower weakens," and after she'd left the store.

He stood behind when she admired the pearls in the display mirror, where she was really modeling herself. All he could do, not to stroke her. As with the girl in the DairyMart, though different emotions and different impulses, Jared balled his fists in his pants pockets. He leaned forward on his toes, allowed himself to breathe in the scent of Pauline's hair. Not fruit, but spice – rich earth and cinnamon.

As he grew to know her, Jared saw she had a way of announcing how she interpreted the world and he waited on her outlook, anticipating it jibing with his, hoping for unity.

She said, "What's true is only true the moment it's spoken. Tomorrow it might not apply." He looked at her, expecting more, or elucidation.

"The heart can't be trusted," she said.

"Come on, Pauline. Heart is all there is."

"Then let's say *another's* heart is not to be trusted."

Jared's sense of the floor supporting them shifted.

Probation was a way of serving a sentence outside of confinement, in which the defendant agreed to obey the "conditions." They called leaving the county without permission absconding.

Pauline pitched Jared in wobbly orbit around her lovely planet. She stood outside his car in the aftermath of her husband's surprise-home visit, the surprise of *them*, as if she didn't fall within either of their claims, no matter how she tried. He'd felt the same with the Tattoo Guy in the DairyMart.

Came a time when words couldn't frame desire, or contain it, when reason erased thought, moments in which man and woman were more animal than divine. He'd watched her hand curled and reaching for the Pontiac's door handle, but also suspended, paused between him and her husband.

Then he'd barreled down the gravel, left her with the choice, for when she dared approach it, when her hand could tighten around the metal and her thumb punch the button, and thereby open him up.

Kansas peeled away into Colorado under his fast driving, foot heavy on forget, his accelerated absconding. There'd be hell to pay, and the predicted considerable grief.

Someone Said Fail

Dusk flattened Pauline's house against the hill. Opposite from Tom on the front porch she watched the world's depth and color fade, felt herself, too, going two-dimensional. Her arms enveloped where her bottom ribs left off. Hugging that gaunt part of her, she said, "My belly burns."

Tom shot back, "So your sneaking's spurred an ulcer now, huh?"

He ducked inside the darkened house before she could hit him with something equally smart. Smarts had eluded her of late, the way bringing Jared home like he belonged here was not smart. Three where two should have stood as her lover and her husband collided that morning in the kitchen.

Tom home unannounced, early; Tom, who nickel-and-dimed her affection. And Jared, whose rain kept her right, his love no trickle, but a shower. The two of them, their clamor and claims, had roasted Pauline as the fire did St. Joan. Far from smart, love made her stupid, and consequently, she burned.

No one damaged, no one bloodied, but their shoves and

twisting and swift, incisive words tore her up. The men had thrashed it out while she, mostly silent, walked the tightrope of their argument. Tom stayed, despite betrayal, and Jared drove off, left her nursing what felt like a cannonball in her gut.

Pauline sat across from her husband at the kitchen table, smoking and watching the smoke trying to flee as night wormed in. The whole day had slid, obliterated mealtimes. Cold breakfast coffee filled their cups. To Pauline's lips, everything tasted stale.

"Do you want something to eat?" she said.

"Do you?"

"I just told you—"

Tom waved at her and her unfinished sentence. "Ain't got much appetite," he said.

She thought food might make her feel better.

Tom read from the newspaper in the half-dark. "Neal Bone's band is playing."

Pauline said, "Turn on a light, you'll ruin your eyes."

He tipped his chair's two rear legs, reaching to the switch.

She rummaged through the utility drawer for tornado candles.

"Don't drag those out," Tom said.

"I want to." She lit three, puddling some wax on saucers for anchoring. Once she shut off the electric, she sat back and admired how Tom looked blessed by candlelight.

"Always playing with fire," he said.

She shrugged. "I can't help what satisfies me."

"It says Boner starts at ten. No opening act," Tom said.

Pauline tilted one candle by its saucer and dripped wax on the table and on the back of her hand, on the edge of the newspaper and atop the veins jumping on Tom's forearm as he drummed his fingers.

"Hey, stop. That shit hurts."

"Does it?" She spoke dreamily.

"You know it does."

Pauline observed the wax on her like a second skin.

"Do you want to go?" Tom said.

Pauline shrugged. "Sure."

"To hear Neal, your first love."

"That's old news."

"Yup," Tom said, "got you a new flame now."

She shoved away from the table and went out in the yard to brush her beloved Pendleton, generating around her a circle of dog hair, gossamer and floaty in the dark. Jared had fled yet remained knotted in her center. She thought: It's come to this –he's turned his face. And you could endure his back if only you knew eventually he'd pivot to you.

She never supposed he'd really go, or really let *her* go.

"I've got one idea how to find him," she whispered in Pen's ear. "Zigzagging all across the West in his brother's Pontiac, he'll have two days on us."

Tom called from the porch, "Pauline?" Then, upon locating her, "So why don't we go down to Eli's?"

"Why don't we?" she said back at him. "But after I'm done."

Tom flipped his hand as he turned to go inside. "Always with that damned dog."

Eli's Lounge was a smoky pit and everybody there loved the smoke, they contributed to it, they sucked it in and blew it out, they increased it, and they increased with it. A crowd packed in as the Neal Bone Band squealed and razzed through its pre-gig tune-up. At the bar, Tom ordered Pauline a Corona.

His sister Fiona elbowed her way through a wall of guys and gals in leather or denim. Fee wore her customary bar-hopping black, '50s beatnik costume, everything but the beret. Pauline bit down on a remark about how tights might not be the girl's most flattering choice. She really had no ax to grind with Fee, as Fiona stealing Neal away was such of the past. Pauline's love life had been Neal, then Tom, then Jared.

The progression of men in less than four years made her sound, even in her own thoughts, like a predator or a flake. What was Pauline without her men?

Fiona clinked her beer bottle against Pauline's and said, "I see you're dressed to the nines."

Pauline touched the pearls at her throat. "Special occasion, right? Boner back in town. Scene of the crime, full circle, all that crap."

"He's just playing a gig, Pauline. It doesn't mean anything to him about you or me."

"Doesn't it?" She needled Fiona, mostly to see what Tom would do about it. She felt rootless, as if she didn't know her own mind, her own heart.

Tom raised his bottle and started calling, "Bone, Bone, Bone," until the whole place and its walls rocked with the chant. He winked at Pauline and she could see him self-satisfied with instigating this something that took off so all-the-world-alive. What neon from the bar could be caught in Tom's eyes glinted there. The light managed to amp up his handsomeness. How the low glow accumulated in him – this had been one of the first elements of Tom that attracted her. Again an unanchored feeling buzzed through, a feeling of question and need and the place to put it all.

Where was she connected, and why? She thought about electrical impulses that stirred or staggered a person. She swallowed a mouthful of beer, stood straighter as she touched her throat, and at the pearls which were fake, of course, because nothing really valuable emerged from the Goodwill piles.

Tom had said, "What you find there are cast-offs, everyone knows that."

He'd once been as much a thrift store supporter as Pauline. Had Tom known before this morning that she gambled there with Jared? At the Goodwill jewelry counter, she played the game every girl learned in junior high, acting like she couldn't care less, acting like Jared wasn't standing behind her, enticed by her. But honest to God she hadn't been angling for a gift, or if she had been, it was more for Jared than for any bought thing. Opening the box he later presented her, she'd wanted to run the beads across her teeth the way she'd seen gypsies and street thieves in movies test for authenticity. She'd wanted to bite the pearls, she wanted to bite him. Once the band launched into their opening set, Eli's became the screech and thump of a thousand hearts, one extended scream. The decibels made behind Pauline's eyes hurt.

Tom sidled up without her noticing until his hip bumped hers. His free arm cradled her shoulder while he gestured his bottle to somebody, then with his mouth to her ear, he said, "Neal's gotten older and louder." Next, he whispered, and his whisper was a magnet that made her lean in to hear. "But not us, Pauline, babe. Not us, not old, not yet."

It was their shared secret from way back: the inky perception that someone, anyone – a dad, a lover, a husband – could wreck you with something stupid out of his mouth.

Tom said, holding her body close, "Our start and our finish line."

Was that an apology or was he putting her on notice? Pauline lowered her head to her beer, felt like a tall bird bent with its beak at a desert watering hole.

"I am old," she told Tom, "as old as Neal Bone."

Tom said, "You and me and Neal are the same age."

She nodded. "Time for plenty more screw-ups."

The band's end note held the space and the crowd erupted all around it, and around the betrayals Pauline and Tom had brought to the bar. Tom wouldn't break his stare. He was on top of her, daring her. The place was body against body and barely air to breathe.

Their bikes had skidded over the years of adolescence, right into Eli's, right on through.

Tom had loved her after the debacle of Neal; he'd given her back her worth. He'd married her.

Why didn't that, now, mean more to her?

Fiona, flush-faced and voice-croaky, broke in. "Is he not as wild as ever?"

"He is," Pauline said.

Tom was not letting her go.

Leaving did not rely on another's letting go, Jared would remind her.

She finally looked away from her husband. "And you know what?" Pauline said. "We should talk with him, Fee, at the break. For old times, and catch up, all that."

Fee's eyes heated with stage light, behind-the-bar-light, all the cigarette lighters popping on. "You think?"

"Sure," Tom said. "Connecting with your past will be good for both you ladies. See up close the wreck you survived." The band started a new number. Tom released them to Neal, then the crowd sucked him in.

Fiona leaned her head to Pauline's. "Tom never liked Neal."

Pauline said, "He doesn't like anybody he hasn't handpicked." And then she felt it swoop over her like the biggest blackbird from on high, a welt of an idea – that she'd been handpicked by Tom, picked like an ear of corn and stuffed into his sack. She didn't know what to do with such knowing.

She adjusted her purse strap on her shoulder, tucked the bag part between her ribs and her elbow, ready to walk the gauntlet to the stage. She said to Fiona, "Ready to find that rocker?"

The stage, that crazed place, drew Fiona and Pauline like the moths they were, to the light, to the light. No longer groupies, but the buzz and the brouhaha still enthralled them. They had each been a part of it at one time or another, Pauline first. First arrived, so first lost.

The guys put down their instruments and started off in search of a smoke, a drink, a soft hip to lean into. Pauline's used to be one of those hips. She'd lost a few pounds since she and Neal split. Only in the last year, she could admit that, yes, he'd dumped her. And when had she been able to own this? When Tom.

But the guitar man had a way of stringing her along and stringing her up and tangling her. So much so, she didn't want Fiona to see, wanted this to be just Neal and her, demonstrating his hangnail still stuck in a soft part of her. She'd written some of Neal's songs, numbers his band played, no doubt a few on tonight's set list.

"What do you think we went to court over?" she'd told Jared just last night. "How do you think I bought this place?"

This seemed of another life, when her lover shrugged there in the dark, rocking dangerously on the back legs of a chair not meant for tilting, his boots a-creaking on the warped boards of her front porch.

"Well, too, I grow some plants up there on the hill." She waved in the direction back of the house, right through the shadowy front door. "Interspersed with the tall weed and the Queen Ann's Lace, the pokeberry and the briars."

Jared's mouth formed a slow, sly smile she could sense more than see as he drew out her name. "Paul-leen, my lovely. Contraband?"

She said, "There's a little illegal in us all."

How would she know where to begin to trail after him? Some once-conversation pointed him west to where his brother Sten had been stationed because he'd talked of the states he'd have to travel through – a bed game he'd played with Pauline in which they characterized the states, back and forth, free associatively.

Kansas.

Jared: "Tornado."

Pauline: "Dorothy."

Jared: "Fortunes."

Pauline: "Red shoes, glittery."

Jared: "Hog slop."

Pauline: "No place like home."

Jared: "The Jayhawks."

Pauline: "Wheat that goes on forever."

Colorado.

Jared: "Skiing."

Pauline: "The Rockies."

Jared: "Grizzlies."

Pauline: "Honey." She smiled.

Jared: "Cold."

Pauline: "Fire." Then she said, "Are we always going to be opposites?"

"Californy," Jared said. Then he said, "Sten."

Pauline: "Hollywood."

Jared: "Sten."

Pauline: "The Pacific."

Jared: "Sten."

Pauline said, "Will you quit?"

"He's all that fills my mind."

She propped herself up on her elbow. God, but Jared looked lovely against the strict white sheets, his hair a curly mess of brown he pushed back from his face and held there with one hand.

"You must have loved your brother to his guts."

"He was my brother and he was me."

He took a break from his maudlin self for a minute and observed her across the small valley in the mattress with a sweet, inscrutable expression. "The dip that hides your eyes drives me crazy, you know that?"

"Yeah." She smiled. She did like to flirt behind that hair. She was in charge of herself, no other way to declare it. She posed herself in the bed exactly so as to entice him.

Then dark clouded the moment. He said, "You hide behind that hair."

She knew what he was on about and she was sick of Sten's memory tripping him, tripping *them* up. "You hide behind your brother."

"You can always cut your hair."

"Yeah, and your brother's dead."

Jared nearly roared, "Nobody's said so."

"Well, lost then," she said. "Missing."

Pauline could not even now describe how that set Jared closed like a ready fist. Serious scuffle. She wondered how long it would be until he hit her. Already she was resigned to the outcome.

It had been their first argument. They hardly ever clashed. With Pauline, Jared moved more than tenderly, not brash as Tom, not distracted as Neal. With Pauline, he was *with* Pauline.

She was wise enough to know this "presence" of his as rarity.

Neal looked at Fiona, then let his gaze slide over to rest on Pauline, his vision a little blank, a little foggy. He was a little messed up, the way required to command Eli's stage, what he called his Starship Enterprise.

He smiled lazy and sighed big and said, "We were a pair, weren't we, Pol?"

Sometimes he'd called her Polly, when he wanted to be affectionate, when he wanted affection.

Neal lifted his cigarette-smoky voice and those nearby paused their drinking to listen to his a capella, "Don't ask who sent you this angel/come in, too, to be my witness/Just love her, love her, love her."

Pauline, slightly embarrassed – but when did embarrassment ever stop her? – looked him directly in the eyes for his go-ahead, then warbled, only so those close could hear, especially Neal because, yeah, she wanted to prove she could still charm him, and she had a pretty sound in her, "You-u-u, my beautiful tattoo/the one I take pain for, and glad the day for /Nothin' can hurt me more than how you hurt me this way."

She'd written both sets of lyrics.

Neal brought her to him in a sweet liquor bear hug. "Hey, Polly," he said into her ear. She drew back to stand on her own glittery ground of the past, full remembering how she'd walked in on Neal and Fiona in the van, when all they'd been hiding became known.

"We were a pair all right," she said. Nothing like the nostalgia pit, she thought. Fascinating, though, how what they three had lived through managed to hone senses tonight dulled by bar light and dimmed by beer.

Neal scratched the back of one long hand with his other's long fingers, the source of all Neal Bone music, agitated in her misreading of him. "No, Pol. I mean good. A good working pair."

Fiona's facial expression had been frozen full of hope for Neal's zeroing in, but Neal's perceptions floated above Fee, on a higher scene, another scale, and partly, yes, caressing Pauline. He had a way of doing that, touch with his eyes. He had a lineup of groupies a mile long. He only had to ask.

The place halfway hushed and the light drew softer when Neal and his band re-took the stage.

"Sheesh. In this dark we'll be bumping each other blind," Tom said. He was already leaning well into Pauline. Where Neal's liquor made him sweet-smelling, Tom had more medicine on his breath.

The techie narrowed a spot on Neal perched with his acoustic atop a bar stool, his long legs wrapped around its legs.

"Become one with the furniture," Tom criticized haughtily into her ear.

Pauline had to admit, Neal milked his act for all it was worth, and Tom called it funny, rightly. She giggled and hit Tom's arm with her empty hand. She'd accepted the next Corona he'd brought her, let him think he was stealing her, but Neal's break was ending when Tom steered her away.

Neal said, picking out a few notes, tuning and refining the tuning as he did, "And I want you all to know this next was written by Pauline Duet, who's here tonight. Pauline?" He squinted into the one light on him that left the others of his band in the shadow.

Smattering of applause and people twisting, turning, craning, trying to find out who is she? Who's got Neal Bone's heart?

Neal didn't need to see her to thank her, she knew all about what he could do with eyes closed.

Pauline stepped a bit toward the vacancy made by the curious crowd mid-stage but floor level, one tier down (Neal always above her). She brought her beer and raised it in tribute to Neal. She brought Tom with her, too, so when Neil kicked the song's first bars, Tom drew her in to dance.

Duet her maiden name, as now she was Pauline Montgomery, wife of the man in whose arms she rocked slowly, heel toe, heel toe.

Tom said, "That asshole."

"Oh, let Neal be for a night. For that matter, let me be, too."

"And so why not let Tom be Tom?" Tom said.

"Do you think we need to talk?" and before he could answer she continued, "You need to let me talk."

Tom said, "Okay."

But then she couldn't cough up the thoughts she'd been mulling for weeks, as in, what does a life of promise mean? Was it this, apparent in the way he held her hips so close to his they were having sex with their clothes on? Tom liked showing that kind of ardor, or just showing off, drawing the buzz to him and using Pauline as the sweet stuff that attracts. Being held by him like this had its pleasures, certainly, but she didn't care for the display.

Mostly, she categorized it as a game. She suspected falsity; and she had her own lies. Jared had told her she was his one and his only, his ever, he'd said so, and that kind of declaration left Tom, with his cynicism, in the dust.

"So it comes down to honesty," Pauline said.

Tom didn't skip a beat. "Okay," he said. "Waiting all day for it."

She hoped he'd go first, but her hopes meant nothing to Tom, who liked to make her squirm. Jared picked up on her hopes, Jared *was* her hope.

Neal sang as Tom and Pauline danced. People made room, skirted around them. They'd grown up in Euphoria, half the bar knew them, even accounting for Pauline's time on the road with the band. And she wrote this ballad they were all worshiping Neal with.

"You used to make me feel so good/Now all you do is bring me pain/At your worst and most broke/There she is again/to lift, to soothe/Bring on yesterday's news/and the shattering, shattering rain/What happened to that part of our bridge?"

Tom had been singing some of the words, too, and spoke the last line into her hair, "Best built things, they sometimes break." Because Neal had gone silent she heard Tom quite clearly.

"We're stronger than that, Pauline. Babe, aren't we?"

She could leave in the face of Tom loving her like this? She shamed herself, she scolded, but she knew she'd be gone by morning.

She'd be back. The place was hers, and hard fought for, that lawyer drag-through with Neal and her rights to her own words. She did not love Neal, maybe had never loved Neal, though she appreciated the chance to see him again as she liked him well enough and adored the ways he adored her when he adored her, when he wasn't adoring himself. She'd liked the life on the road, the rootless world of gigs and off-the-map towns that celebrated you just because you were the newest thing they'd seen in months come across the borders of their little municipalities. Something about wheels humming, and her above, ferrying her to new and better and different, it stirred her up.

Tom and Pauline made it home, as people do, that half miracle that guides all drunks safe to the creaky porch. *Oh, there's the step, watch now, don't touch the light, let's sleep, we'll be all right.* But no one slept. They stretched their fingers in the dark for something they couldn't touch, fumbling in the wide silence that presses in in the wake of a night of loud-played music.

And after, Tom got up, and Pauline lay cast back on the sheet, heard the fridge suck open and closed in the kitchen, and then the crack free of another bottle cap. Tom watched her from the bedroom doorway, his arms bracing the door jambs, one wrist folded so his hand could clutch the beer.

All seemed suspended.

She might have slept, she might have dreamed Tom in the doorway, or maybe only seconds had elapsed since he stood in that same place, the beer bottle still wore sweat, his hair askew from the way her hands had worked through it. Dream or not, she rose and dressed under Tom's observation, which kind of creeped her out and kind of thrilled her. Either way, she wasn't stopping.

She packed panties and jersey pull-on shorts and soft, much-washed tee shirts – comfortable clothes for driving.

"I have to fly," she said.

"Don't tell me you're going after him."

"Lock up the house like you always do. I'll be back. I need to go for now."

"Running is what you're doing, Pauline." Tom called it what it was. Then he said, "Hey, I got my own work calling. I might be heading out myself on Monday."

So they were playing it stoic for now; she could beat the rap on stoic. No one had switched on a close lamp and Tom stood backlit by whatever he'd left burning in the kitchen.

Pauline stopped tucking clothes into the bag's small corners and examined him. "Can't you ever once say what you're feeling?"

"Didn't I? Back in the bar? Wasn't that some heartfelt stuff?"

She remembered their tight-lock dancing, and being embarrassed but not embarrassed enough to quit, or too tired, and maybe enjoying it, the way he rocked her hips with his, the way he'd just done her on this bed. At Eli's there'd been his breath in her ear as he spoke, but what he'd whispered sounded raspy and unforgiving and not made of words she knew. She didn't seek forgiveness anyway, only disappearance.

"You failed," Tom said.

She couldn't believe he was pinning this on her. She said, "We failed each other."

He said, "What about promises we made?"

Her laugh cut and mocked. "Once upon a time?"

He said, "Don't they count?"

She shook her head, which could have been against lots of objections. Did those vows, and Tom's sudden interest, post no strength in the bartering in her head? If this, then that. Because he did, then I will do. Or since he doesn't, why should I?

There sat a small place in her heart Tom would never reach – not that he couldn't try and not that she wouldn't let him in. Could she give him the key? And if she could, beyond that, could she live with him, stay with him, if he never accessed that place? Would nine-tenths be good enough when she knew Jared gave her ten of ten? No, she decided. She zipped closed the tote bag. No.

She ducked under his high held arms, spread as they were, would accept whatever way she'd manage to breeze by him, nothing breezy in it.

He said, pausing her there so his face might meet hers to spit or to kiss, "I'm not caring for your dog, you know." His mouth expelled the stale liquor he'd been sucking down all night at Eli's and now this new fresh beer. Pauline swore she'd return the look as long as it took to get out of there, a stare-down while she swallowed sick.

She said, "I'm taking Pendleton."

"That's the best damn idea you've had all day," Tom said, his voice rising to cuff her back while she walked the hall to the kitchen light she felt she had to put a hand on, to feel the murmur of her house in its electricity and its life, and then to extinguish it.

If You're Feeling Sick

At the bar that held up Jared the wood wept, the glasses wore sweat, the fan above lazed and the door kept it dark. Jared had been sitting there steadily acquiring a slump since God knows when; the sun was still on the move to its zenith, for sure, at his entry. He was tanked.

Still, each time that door squeaked its hinges and shot in the light of the world for just a pause, he thought he saw his angel Pauline walking to him through that bitter bright. He was pissed at her for her absence because he'd specifically asked her to be present. But how could she be expected to know his route, to chase, when she couldn't even come down off her hill?

"Just like Mom, you make it too hard to love you," Sten whispered from the smoky end of the bar. "Impossible hoops to jump through. Man, you got to lighten up, release the fist."

Jared imagined Pauline brushing her dog, eddying the air with dog fluff, Pendleton grinning, his hammerhead lifted into each lovely stroke, leaning into Pauline's long gorgeous legs, her jeans tight across her thighs, and her boots all scuffed up from playing in the remnants of the cut-up tree. That storm had crashed through and what a difference in temperature, in high pressure, in lassitude. Or did he mean altitude?

Of course, Jared sat so far from Euphoria, Illinois, that the desert wind was buffing his toenails. He lowered his head and peered into the gloom under the bar where his feet resided.

Boots. Still shod. Figure of speech then, that toenail stuff.

Paul-leen. His mind could wail in perfect silence. He'd perfected the perfect silence years ago under his mom's temperamental flick of the wrist, swat from the elbow, and under the tutelage of Sten's tough brother love. Nobody bothered saying what they really wanted, how they really felt. It was a game of camo and don't let your face tell your truth.

He promised himself if he found a woman deserving, he would throw all of that aside, and he had. He had been so transparent with Pauline he was glass. She would see right through Glass Jared to Jared's glass heart, easily shattered, and which he had kept from all, in wait for her. Of course he hadn't secured it; it'd been split and cut and splintered and almost melted. He could never wall it off. Protection was beyond his abilities. He couldn't protect anybody. He didn't know what he'd been thinking, supposing such romantic bullshit.

Sten had pronounced about their rough-and-tumble childhood, "When we learn from our history, the memories will fade."

But it looked like Jared had more to learn because his past loomed as present as ever. It laid its film over the now, clouding his future, warping his dreams. He didn't know if he could cross the California border. He didn't know if

Sten's Pontiac would make it; it was leaking oil like a sieve.

He didn't know if his heart could be this far from Pauline and still knock out a beat.

"Hell," he said. "Where is she?"

"She, who?" the bartender said. There wasn't a woman in the joint.

"I think you've about hit your limit, buddy. Coffee's on the boil, and that's all you'll be getting."

"Yeah," Jared said, "coffee." Again he examined his boots. He felt like he might not lift his head without help of a crane.

Under the direction of murderous brother, Sten, Jared learned to bite back on his desires. He found in wanting them so badly, but quietly, that his want could produce movement in people's lives. He only had to wish hard enough. He'd wished hard for Pauline, past and present.

Sten said, "A woman's tears, you can steel yourself to them, like a shoulder to the wheel, like a job to do, you withstand it."

Then he had to go and spout opposite because logic didn't rule in Ghost World, and this smackdown was theater-izing in Jared's Ghost Town head.

Bartender was wrong when he said, "Ain't no women here." He knew damned well he employed a barmaid, who'd been in the back punching open the clean laundry sack from American Linen with a steak knife. She brought a few towels crisp with their industrial sanitizing and hung them behind the bar near the huge stainless gully of an ice tub attached there.

She couldn't help but see Jared. Jared grew out of the bar like the tall trees in California, as if he'd been there since God created, as if he'd been a little acorn now all grown to oak. He tried to stand.

Axis, axle, ankle, all tilted most dangerously.

She caught hold of his elbow and steadied his ass down. "Honey, you might want to sit and stay awhile." She refreshed his coffee, percolated a smile. "Got a couple quarters? I'll punch some jukebox numbers for you. The band won't show for another hour."

"Hour might as well be death," Jared said.

She pursed her lips, disappointed she couldn't rouse him out of his gloom. An up-tempo Bruce or Mellencamp flipped on her Christmas lights. She was an easy girl, a "Little Pink Houses" girl, a "you and me" girl.

"That's just feeling pitiable," she said. "And we won't have it." She poured a cup of coffee for herself and perched on a stool, the bar between them.

Her boss said, "You want a sandwich from Derelict's?"

She waved him away, and the wave morphed into an accusing point at her customer.

"He's the one should eat."

Jared waved, too, listlessly, wristlessly. "Nobody here wants anything."

The man shed his apron, dashed to the door and set the whole place on its stark white ear, and then returned it to the dark.

Jared had lifted his arm to block the obscenity. Still, his eyes watered.

"Sten told me a woman's tears are everything," he said, dipping deeper into his afternoon monologue. "They're you and they're her, too, and they're the reason for crying. You find your tears beside hers, mixing in both your ears, lying there together on the bed, they block the intruding world."

"Sten who?" the girl said.

So she learned about his brother the missing, his

brother the dead, his brother with one gun for shooting doves and another for Afghans, all fucked-up wisdom and cartoon guts. "Who joined the band of brothers shit," Jared said. Then he bellowed, "*I* was his brother!"

"Sure," the barmaid said. She'd seen worse. This guy was not so bad. She could take this guy upstairs and eat him like candy.

Sten, whose shade haunted the bar's cashier-end where the girl had stacked all her empty checks, said, "Words are their own dope, especially for folks like us, eh, bro? We swallow them fast as they're spoke. Pure delusion. I mean stupid, the way they stew our blood. Words and fucking women."

"Right," Jared said. He was dreaming of Pauline. He thought he saw her standing behind the formidable ledge where he leaned his elbows and thus the weight of his sluggish upper body.

Her hair reflected sun off all the dazzly bottles even with night coming on. Pauline's lips held back a bevy of words his tongue had mixed with.

"You got quarters?" the barmaid said.

"Wanna dance?" Jared said, standing, digging coins out of his jeans' pockets. He thought he could do it if someone held him up.

"A Whiter Shade of Pale" moved them into each other. Seasick, yes, and the room it did hum. His mouth felt like cardboard.

Pauline had told him, perched above him like a big white bird, the loveliest of doves his Pauline, "When I give I give big, I give all. I give like it can't ever come back, I give like divorce. Permanent."

She'd unbuckled him and her hands feathered his skin. She was his, her breath across his hips, then sharper. He knew her and she knew him like no other. His eyes were closed but he could feel them rolling back in his head, his head nodding and his murmuring, unintelligible, no words, just what she drew from a place deep in him that rarely felt light, vibration, or air, that rarely felt right.

Pauline was miles away, states away, on her gravel hill, tending plants and writing poetry she'd turn into songs and petting her dog's ears instead of his. Jared had his hands on the bar maid's hips, and she hugged him close, out of necessity. She was a pool of any liquor he wanted, all he had to do was give her a sign. He smelled the Tanqueray and the Jack, he took it with a twist.

She said, "You're rocky, buddy."

His hands freed her and went to his hair. He grabbed it back from his face, pulling his scalp tight and slow, groaned. He said, "I should be shot."

"Not with the guns again."

"I got to piss," he said.

She said, "I got customers," paused for him to object, and when he didn't, they divided.

The jukebox glow showed her hair didn't dare approach Pauline's honey. Drinkers had arrived. The band straggled in, bringing smoke and sweet air and instruments to get through the night.

"Hey, Sandy," one of them said. "Set us up, would ya?"

Jared thought of Pauline's contraband on the hill, wondered how he could get back to her there, and about what the law could do to him. He felt he had been set up by the bartender who ducked out to dinner and by dance-with-me-Sandy, by the months-ago Tattoo Guy and the deputy and the girl with the Salems.

But he wouldn't call his brother deserter, or betrayer, not yet. He vowed to keep moving west, to cross the

California line and see if it made any damned difference. Jared punched through the door of the men's room and gave away all that had been flowing and let loose in him.

What was the name of this town? This bar? He had to find a room before he broke down dead.

Crick in the neck, arm twisted funky in lost circulation, feet dangly out the window, socks wet with night. Sometime Jared must have kicked off his boots. He moved his eyeballs slowly around to assimilate what comprised the dark. Ball bearings ground in rotation in his skull.

Bed was the Pontiac's back seat; at least he hadn't done damage behind the wheel. Fact: he couldn't set his hands on the car keys to ignite.

He worked his dead fist back to life, brought both his arms below his head to increase blood flow. And the dreams returned, competed.

"You like this baby?" Sten said. They must have been flying a good seventy-five down the highway, four windows full open, the summer reaching in like a lover risen out of the lake, night-wet and tasty. Two brothers, playing Chuck Berry, with no particular place to go. Maybe pick up some girls. U.S. military in the future's arms, Al Qaeda still training in their Afghan caves.

"What's not to like?" Jared said. Even the way he flicked his cigarette he picked up from Sten: Observe and learn, little brother. He flicked it now and ash blew into the back seat.

"She's yours then. Don't set her on fire."

"Mine?"

"Can't take the car. Army don't have me a parking space."

Protest aimed to claw out of Jared's throat, but Sten already sported his military haircut.

"Deal done."

Jared said, "I'll keep her 'til you get back. A loaner."

Sten bore a deadly meaningful look into him there across the front seat, his pupils so big and deep and dark with something he'd swallowed besides six-pack fuel. "Do this for me," he said. In the too long look, he drove right off the road.

Boys they were again, but trapped in wrecked steel and heat and smoke and flesh. They were nothing but their bones, they were melting to skeletal. The boys bled and the dream bled with them.

Driving with Pauline now. Again on the highway. Always, with Jared, a long stretch of road.

"You're cruising into the other lane," she said, hyper in her voice. His lazy Pauline, all hepped-up-touchy and criticizing his steadiness.

He didn't like driving and arguing at the same time. Since both needed one hundred percent Jared, both suffered. He was supplying excuses.

"I was on probation," Jared said. "And unemployed, about to lose my place. You caught me weak, Pauline. I was vulnerable."

That car could have combusted on the spot the way the fire and ire rose up out of her.

"YOU were the vulnerable one? Don't make me sound like a bird of prey. Was you who ambushed me at the end of the sidewalk."

"Come on, Pauline. We've both been guilty of stalking in the Goodwill."

"Checking out," she said, "maybe. Looking for bargains, right? But you were the one who insisted. You pushed. You toppled me. Your take is mistaken. I was the one vulnerable." She started crying.

"Okay, we both were too open to something. Something good, right? Okay? Just shush, Pauline, shh." He tried reaching across to stroke her hair; he didn't know what else to do with this woman turned phoenix, who depended on him and for whom he had no answers, only nightmares about what loving could lead to.

"Oh, our fights make us boring," she said. She slumped grumpy, her streaked, lovely face far from his reach, retreated against her passenger door. Her head tilted back the way some pose to apply eye drops, Pauline blinking past her tears.

Jared traveled with them, according to gravity, along that downy skin, from the plane of cheek toward the opening of her whisper-fine ears, desire igniting his Pontiac world. He took a too-fast turn, launched Pauline to mix it up with Sten in the tangled, mangled car.

Tap, tap, tap. The barmaid peered through the open back window over his feet.

"You okay?"

"Hmm," he half-groaned. His mouth tasted ash, his head swelled with poison. His body still hummed from the road.

Sandy said, "You're going to be all kinked up. Upstairs you could stretch out. Promise I won't jump you. I've got a couch and a floor. You choose." Smudged eyeliner, after the long shift she'd worked, made her a raccoon. It must have been three in the morning, maybe later. The halogen flooding the parking lot made everything look eaten up by acid and on the other side of death.

"Yes," he said, clearing his throat. "Yes," he repeated through rising grit. His loved ones' dreams fled as he struggled out of the back seat. He unfolded, he gathered, he pulled himself into one person the best he could. The night air was soft and balmy for September in Colorado. She wound up all his windows, then she worked his feet into his boots.

"Stand," she said. "Stomp."

She slipped her arm around him, cool and damp, held him tight at his waist and stumbled him to her apartment. Jared thought it would be okay because they were stepping up, she was helping him walk. They were ascending, right? And wasn't into hell always called The Descent? So he figured going up was positive, was saving. She wasn't Pauline, but maybe she was an angel, too. He sputtered a laugh that tasted like butane, that could have incinerated if they'd lit a match.

"What's funny?" Sandy said.

"Like I could sleep and not dream," he said.

"You're drunk-talking," she said. "Step up here."

After working the key, she tried pushing the lower panel with her leg not supporting Jared but the door was warped and needed a good slug. She punched full with her body, dragged his weight along, too, and they pitched in onto the apartment floor, the carpet taking a layer off Jared's elbow. The parking lot glare, and the bar below's neon, colored the see-thru drapes enough for Jared to pick up the apartment's Mexican-Western décor. A serape covered the couch cushions. A ceramic Pedro with his donkey attached to a cart of flowers sat atop a huge console television. That TV must have been fifty years old. In an upstairs apartment like this, on the edge of the nation's middle, where time and fads stuck like briars as much as they swept through like tumbleweed, it seemed normal.

"Nice place," Jared said.

They lay on their backs beside one another, after the forced entry. She only needed to turn her head to look him in the eyes, and she did.

"It's all right," she said. "All I can afford, for now. A lot of Goodwill." She tucked some of her hair behind her ear and it fell right back to cross-eyeing her. She said, "But I plan changes."

Sten, lurking in the still-dark kitchen said, Ain't that what it's about, changes?

You plan, you hope, you dream some. But all you really got is now, Jared thought.

Plan all you want, Sten said. Only action's gonna get you there to the bird, to the goal, to the girl. This girl, that girl – what's the difference?

"I don't know," Jared said. That was a lie; he did know. The difference ran a river through him and spoiled him for anybody other than Pauline.

Not interested in her changes, Jared was establishing his own. He sat, pleased to be upright, to bend his knees for someplace to hook the length of his arms, fearing they might wander over to embrace her, the Sandy option still not eliminated.

He rubbed at and scratched his nose like he was preventing a sneeze. "My nose smells sick," he said.

"You need some Tylenol and about a gallon of water." She started to hike her purse up her shoulder, but he relieved her of it. He took care of that hair that kept falling into her eyes.

He tried kissing and she tried back, all encouragement, with tongue, the two of them reclining. He accepted it for what it was, which was not Pauline. After she was done experimenting Jared curled politely into himself, to stop himself, to halt whatever had got started.

He said, "I'm still pretty tanked."

Sandy mimicked his body language to make it appear she'd been declining all along.

"Yup," she said. "You're looped. Let me get that water." She arrived at her height in stages, and looking up at her he thought, she's a damned tall girl.

You knew that from dancing with her, Sten said.

But Jared did not remember dancing.

Sandy plunked her shoulder bag on the counter with her keys. She made noise in the cupboards, ran the faucet, cracked ice.

Was it kind of crazy they continued operating in the dark? Jared didn't think it was his place to switch on a light. His vision had adjusted despite this thick-headed feeling. He didn't deem Sandy poor or deficient or the surroundings paltry. He was clear of judgment because he was mired in the Goodwill world he and Pauline had erected, and which he maintained in his head, a kind of torture and guiding beacon. He simply had no other interest.

Sandy hit the light above the stove. It made the kitchen look lit from below. The linoleum out there must have been white or reflective. Because of it, she could be as ghostly as Sten. Or maybe all Jared was prepared to meet were ghosts, things that would not last.

Sandy rubbed at her eyes. She said, "I'll leave this on so you don't stumble. The bathroom's at the end of the hall. If you're feeling sick, please use it, okay? I don't want to wake up to mop up." She came around the counter and handed him a full Big Gulp cup.

"Thanks." He could still direct his politeness and his winning smile to good things offered him.

She disappeared down the hall.

After drinking big, he zeroed in on the couch. He embraced it, and the serape, too. He dreamed of Mexico, true dream, for he'd never been, and never would. Mountains, desert, coast and canyons. No foreign countries; California was as foreign as he'd fly. Different kind of weather, different kind of landscape. Twelve shades of blue you can't imagine in Euphoria pressed flat-to-pristine in that California light.

Sten promised, "A new vision, bro, just come on out here. But soon. Don't wait 'til I'm dead, huh?"

Jared, always delaying or jumping the gun. That's how he'd arrived here, hopeless, aching for Pauline, on another woman's deviant springs, in a place he still didn't know the name of, unable to find his way.

Pauline inhabited his mind, she never left. Shit. She'd been present all along, and what he'd been begging her to show him, she'd demonstrated countless times. He was a spoiled prick, sweeping her from his car, him blasting out of Euphoria, logging hundreds of miles between them, putting on her the need to prove, him expecting her grand gesture, all the while he drove pleading with the horizon for a sign the way the Egyptians watched the sky for their next plague, asking of Pauline decision – not an impulse like her stowaway in the back seat, but thought-through and deliberate – a move that would show her heart would abide with his.

She was his compass, she was *his* way, she was the tide returning. He only asked that she leave Tom, and that the flight be her choice, undiluted by his need. But he saw now, not possible, because he and Pauline knotted up like a double helix that not one or the other, *no one*, could tease out.

Read the Map

As to the issue of cell phones, Pauline didn't have one. Tom's, for business, tittered the first notes of "Temptation Eyes," an opening beyond which Pauline rarely heard because her husband stifled his phone's music, whispered into it his indecipherable answer. The one on the line knew what was said. The one calling knew Tom was sneaking. And then he tried making light of it.

"Phone's my business card, my future gig, our next meal," he told Pauline. She shouldn't mess with it, didn't need to know the who, the why, or the wherefore.

"Maybe I need my own."

"Pauline, honey, what do you need a phone for?"

"Emergencies?" She could conjure a few.

"Honey, the landline's enough. I'm who's on the road." He treated her like a child who couldn't possibly catch on.

"And keep your hands off my shit," he said. She had no business scrolling through numbers rung, numbers called in, numbers on speed dial. No earthly reason why his phone should even be in her hands. As if she, not he, had something to hide. And, conversely, he didn't give a shit what she thought or where she went or what she thought about where he went. She lived with diabolical twins.

As to the issue of cell phones, Jared didn't have one. He barely kept ahead with his efficiency, and an efficient manner of living. He ignored his bills, cut up credit cards, slammed solicitors, vowed he'd not be beholden. He was a little paranoid about being tracked. Pauline was unaware he'd been thinking of packing his few possessions and calling his next residence a room at the YMCA.

Nobody said traveling with a dog would be easy. Pendleton rode tall in the passenger seat, head lifted out the window. As a teenager, somebody told Pauline dogs loved doing that because air rushing at great speed through their noses got them high.

"No ideas of jumping," Pauline said. She knew how being high could make you act kooky.

The dog looked at her the way Tom often did, a short measure, then Pendleton returned to sucking his wind.

Not the dog so much worrying her, as the surge and hang-up of the car when her foot plunged the gas. The Bonny had a Cadillac engine. The salesman who peddled it to her used had said, "Zero to sixty in sixty seconds." This sell-slogan, his abracadabra mantra enticed, and now she was stuck. But no, not stuck; she loved the Bonneville, paid for with her first royalties check before she'd even considered herself squared enough to buy her own house or her own land, which she also did with the settlement money.

What else was difficult: eating from the drive-thru, maintaining the straight drive, keeping spillage from her lap while avoiding Pendleton's vigilant chops. The dog would snatch that meal right out of her hand if she blinked wrong. "Good boy, stay, stay, stay." She watched his eyes, his snout practically in her ear. She let him lick her fingers after, and found baseline joy in the warm, wet reverence of the animal.

"God knows your failures and loves you anyway," read the highway billboard advertising one of the dozens of small-town churches she drove past. May be sacrilege, but she substituted "Jared" for "God," "Jared knows your failures and loves you anyway," and she had a sense of being seen straight to her pitiful core. So why couldn't she have bid Tom his sorry goodbye and come alongside Jared on his flight? Because this wasn't something to share. Jared's flight was *on him,* it was his own. His own choice, his own consequence. And she couldn't help him bear it. She should have known this before, but her love hid what she didn't wish to see.

Through the rest of Illinois and long across Kansas she passed through towns of faith and dangled hope: Sugar Grove; Word of Faith Ministries; Faith Mountain Ministries; Pica Valley; Praise & Glory Tabernacle; Painted Creek; Slowly Creek.

She wanted to understand what drove Jared, why he went off the way he did. Mostly she was spooling her anger about being left behind, about having few clues, about his arrogance and his easy discard of her. Hundreds of miles logged on this tank of gas in his supposed direction, and she felt she'd been a fool to believe that with him she could change her life.

He'd fucking left her, told her to get out of the car until she could be "present." No use resurrecting the hurt, or the questions she'd bashed him with and he refused to answer. He could be a quiet man when he wanted. What good could come of talking about what they'd already talked to death? Thing was, new questions, especially all along this long drive, were always popping in her mind, new flashbulb pleas, the "hey, what about this when you said that and we shared XYZ?" New mazes with centers overgrown.

Jared's facts differed. Not lies, not warped, just skewed, a different point of view. Because she had the honest take on what had been between them, didn't she? The stumbling block seemed to be he'd wanted her to leave Tom. Well, look here, Jared. Look who left.

You don't need this man's test, his proving ground, she told herself. And still she continued, with a shaky foot, wary of something not quite right with the engine. She cursed Tom for dissuading her from getting a cell phone.

By nightfall, her eyes burned from the watchfulness of nine-plus hours on asphalt. She'd wanted to reach where I-70 bent northwest before quitting. She wanted to make it to Goodland, or better yet cross the Colorado line, but she stopped for the night in a town called Angelus.

In the hotel room, Pauline unfolded the map and spread it on the floor next to a plastic glass of half Coke and half rum, which she felt she deserved. Actually, she was sipping her second.

"Because look how far we've already come," she said to Pendleton. The dog's eyes shifted left and right to watch her swooping, demonstrating hand, but his head remained atop his paws on the bathroom mat she'd dragged to the floor at the foot of this rented double bed.

"You tired? I'm tired, too," she said. She patted him, then rested back on her heels as she knelt.

She drank and zeroed in on the interstate arteries, hoped this one time for Sten's magnetism to win out, trusted it to pull Jared along the most direct route, the fastest road to ruin, Route 70, west all the way to Utah. In Utah, he would make a choice, and Pauline would have to intuit that choice or risk losing track of him.

Not sure he'd head north once he reached Denver and hook up with I-80, or if he'd drive two-thirds of Utah then go up to Salt Lake that way. Either or, she was sure he aimed at San Fran and not LA. They'd talked about the Bay Area's fog.

She'd said, "You can stay right here in Euphoria and get your fill of fog most fall mornings."

Fog and that California light, the way Sten had described it, lured Jared like a goddamned Svengali.

"Ha! Svengali," she said.

She lay on the floor, drunk with the dog, atop the spread open United States. The rum made her ask, What could her life be now? Why did she want a man who ran from her?

A piece of possible song drifted through her mind: How easy to say those things you say/when you're miles away/and merely dream and merely sway. I ought to write that down, she thought. Oh, she would in just a minute. She closed her eyes and felt the floor biting at her bones before she felt nothing.

In the middle of the night, she tore off her clothes and crawled between bedsheets that felt like parchment. I'm a letter in an envelope, she thought. Pendleton leaped onto the bed and settled in. Then she slung her arm around her dog and slept.

Morning brought pounding on the door and the apologetic "Housekeeping." At which time the phone rang. "The desk, Miz Montgomery. Wondering if you're planning to be with us another night?"

Her sleeping through checkout put Pauline another twelve hours behind Jared.

"He must be in California by now," she said.

"Beg your pardon?"

She held the desk on the phone. "Can you give me an hour's grace?"

"Certainly. If it's an hour is all."

First, she got Pendleton out the door to lift his leg. And then she burst through a furious shower, dress, pack up, and key return.

The Bonneville took its time turning over, but it revved to life, and balancing a fix-it-yourself coffee from the motel "breakfast" counter, Pauline was once again winging her way west.

At least the sun hit the back of her neck.

Her head ached, her teeth clamored and her belly growled for something to set digestive juices into. She endured an hour and a half before she pulled off the highway, needing to pee. With a double shot of espresso and a muffin in her belly and a banana for the road, she returned to the car. The car refused to light up. She'd been ignoring the *check engine* indicator for the last two or three hundred miles.

She shoved her sunglasses on top of her head. "Okay, where are we, Pen?" She dragged open the map, and with a right and left glance, examined her rest stop surroundings. She re-tried the car. The map said she was west of Goodland, closer to a town named Pitiful. She laughed at that, laughed 'til she cried and then she wiped her eyes. She turned the key but got nothing. She thought of the emergency cell phone Tom had discouraged.

"I'm alone on the fucking plains of Kansas," she yelled.

With all the windows open, she attracted a few stares. She stopped short of giving the lurkers the finger. She sat in the driver's seat of her dead car, touching the pearls at her neck she'd been wearing non-stop, even in the shower and when she slept, since Neal's hometown comeback two nights ago. Not for Neal did she wear them; was Jared who'd gifted them. On account of Jared, she wore them.

"Actually, I wear them for myself," she told Pendleton, "because I look pretty with pearls at my throat." She recalled viewing herself in the mirror at Goodwill, when the pearls were a wish.

Her dog served as her audience. She snapped on his leash and said, "Let's go, baby," intent on snagging the rest stop phone ... what? Call home? Tom? Oh, she'd decide once she dropped some coins in, once the operator asked who to charge.

All kinds of people mingled around Pauline, and scattered to the drinking fountain, to the candy machines, to the restrooms, to the blow-up map of the nation's middle plastered along the southern wall of the rest stop. Pauline wanted to absorb the cool of this cavernous room before she lifted a receiver and called anywhere. She felt heated in her clothes and under her arms and at the base of her throat. She still didn't know what number she would dial.

A cherub-faced man standing at her elbow and studying the map as hard as she, said, "You look troubled."

She thought he said, "You looking for trouble?" a pickup line that would pitch her right over the edge of this shaky late morn.

She squinted at the map and purposely did not divert her gaze. "I'm perfect, thank you." She studied the border between Kansas and Colorado, which appeared adjacent to the "You are here" arrow.

The guy smelled like Old Spice, an aftershave for dads and grandfathers though he couldn't have been over thirty, hairline receding some at the temples, but otherwise youthful in a choirboy sort of way. She observed the ruddy cheeks, the fresh-scrubbedness of the ensemble he wore –

madras shorts and a blue golf shirt, no socks and serious running shoes. Pauline bet his fancy footwear contained all the newest cushioning Nike had developed.

"It's just that you seem, I don't know, lost," he said. He crossed his arms over his chest. Pauline would have sent the same non-invasion sign but she had Pendleton's leash to hold.

"Gorgeous dog of yours," he said.

"Thanks." She saw the guy's eyes were swampy and red-rimmed.

His arms opened their defense and he bent into a squat to pet Pendleton. "Had a German Shepherd when I was growing up. In St. Louis." Which he didn't have to say. He didn't have to share his anything with Pauline.

"Pen's got some collie in him, too, I think," she said.

"Pen? Like ... penitent?"

She shuffled through her mind all she had to be sorry for. "Pendleton. Like the wool. I just enjoyed the formality of the name."

"You a formal kind of woman, then?" The guy stood and pointed at her neck. "Oh, these." She touched the pearls. "They make me feel richer than I am. You see I paired them with jeans, so not so formal and not so rich, definitely, no."

The guy's smile faded. He leaned in. "Forgive me if I'm intruding, but you look to me a little at loose ends. You're not from around here?"

"Who in a roadside rest stop is ever from around where they stand resting?"

"Touché. What I'm trying to say is, do you need help?"

"A Good Samaritan in almost-Colorado," Pauline declared. "Or a scam artist." She narrowed her eyes trying to decide.

"Ma'am—"

"Pauline," she said. "I got a thing about being called *ma'am*, which is I don't like it."

He said, "Assistance is my calling."

She burst out laughing. "That's a new one."

"Honest." He held out his hand in introduction. "Father Herron Gallagher."

"Wow. A Catholic priest?" she said.

"Episcopal." He moved close and whispered, "The pope's ne'er-do-well relation."

Pauline tapped her chest. "Methodist."

Herron smiled. "I'll try not to hold that against you. Nor try to convert you. Now, really, if there's a problem, maybe I can help."

They started walking to the door and out to the parking lot.

"You tinker with souls," she said, "but what do you know about machines?"

"Cars. A little."

They stood beside the Bonneville. Pauline said, "She won't start."

He put out a cupped hand for her keys. "May I try?"

Tom would say anybody doing you any favor for free, hop that train, girl. Jared distrusted most everyone he came across. And what did Pauline think? She didn't know. She judged the man and the situation by how her dog sniffed him out. Pendleton sat, grinning as Herron scratched him under his chin. The dog's tail slowly wagged, and Pauline plowed forward.

Of course, the car behaved no better for the reverend, for which she felt foolishly vindicated. Herron raised the hood, tugged at a few wires and lifted a hose, but she figured by his attire alone he didn't know enough to diagnose.

"I can drive you to Perry's Automotive. Was on my way there as it is. Perry'll tow it in and find out the matter."

"Truly?"

"Lock this up and we'll take my car."

Inside his Subaru, Herron swept up CD cases and Power Bar wrappers and a stack of flyers for a night at St. Alban's advertising "Get Focused!"

Pauline had to spring on her toes to climb into the cleared passenger seat, but Pendleton had no problem leaping in. She guided the dog over the console and into the back, where Herron worked shoving aside ledger books and running clothes and bags of stuff, stuff and more stuff. He'd been amazed to learn she was about to use the rest stop phone because she didn't have another way to call for help.

"In this day and age, and you traveling cross-country alone, that's just ludicrous," he said. "The first thing we're going to do after we get your car repair underway is buy you a cell phone."

"How far's Perry's?" She fretted a bit now that she sat in this stranger's car. Could he be a wolf in sheep's clothes? A preppy sheep, a priest sheep?

He said, "About a twenty-minute drive, near my church, on the outside of Pitiful."

Pitiful, meaning, she knew, a town because she'd read it on the map, she put her hand to her mouth but laughed anyway. She couldn't help it. She laughed and she laughed. It struck her as so funny that someone had named the place they lived Pitiful, that it was legally on municipal books and government rolls and birth and death certificates. There was probably a Pitiful Cemetery and a Pitiful Town Hall and a Pitiful Post Office and a Pitiful Elementary. All so pitiful it made her laugh until she cried. Then she keened for a while, with Herron driving quietly and, when he dared, flicking his eyes from the road to her.

Pauline had accepted road loneliness, but she had not spoken with another human being since she'd left Tom, except for the plaid-clad girl she paid at the burger joint, the motel desk clerk, and the disembodied voice at the Gas'n'Go.

She dried her face with her shirt sleeve and sighed and breathed big and loud and long, and swiped the back of her hands at her neck where even the pearls were wet. "Sorry. I didn't mean to make fun of your hometown."

"I'm from St. Louis, I told you. Pitiful's just where I ended up."

Herron's eyes teared, too, and the fact of his tears dried up hers. Was he crying for her? Pauline grew curious about this reverend's St. Louis boyhood and his now Pitiful church. She felt exhausted from the road, and all at once quite unafraid.

She veered from the fact of the man crying for God knows what reason, and petted Pendleton's head almost at rest atop her shoulder. She eyed all the junk pushed to one side of the backseat, including the box for nifty new shoes.

"You're a runner?" she said.

He nodded while driving. "Long time, long distance. I'm not going to win any sprints, but I get the cardio going until I manage to banish all that's bothering me so I can feel good about me again."

"Sounds addictive."

He laughed. "Oh, it is, it is. But safer than drugs, tastier than drink."

"I'd have to concur."

"You run?"

Pauline had been no girl big on activity. In fact, Tom called her a sloth. But Tom didn't know she'd begun a regime with Pendleton up and down the gravel. She wished she had enough money to pave that damned driveway. Ran up the back hill to check on what was growing and what was hidden, Pen ever beside her. And then on the road. Her road, strange roads, any roads. The dog would look up at her with his tongue and his drool, his doggy eyes and his doggy grin asking, Now? Now? Done now? Done yet? He slogged on with Pauline as far as she went, as far as she needed to go.

"Took it up recently," she said. "Like you, I guess, trying to outrun what nags me." She paused. "It's good for that," she said, "until you stop. Trouble is, eventually, you always have to stop."

"We should pair up, push each other. A little competition."

"I don't know. I'm really only beginning. I'd probably slow you down."

"Nah, Pauline, you'd motivate me. I just have this feeling you'd be a spur right where I need it."

She tried catching Herron's eyes to see what sparked behind them, if this was a backdoor way of coming on to her because men in her life had ever slipped in that way, but he wouldn't cut his attention from the road so she, too, looked ahead at all the placid streets they passed, containing all the placid Kansas bread-basket lives. And porches with swings and small plastic chairs anticipating tiny behinds or elf butts or children, sheltered by monstrous trees nobody living had planted, trees that had been growing a long time, trees that had always been.

Like the trees in Euphoria before the weird weather blew through and uprooted them.

She put her fist to her heart, quelling the attractive idea of children, and breathed deeply from outside her window. She said, "I love the smell of spent summer."

Herron said, "Yes." He directed the Subaru over the curb. "Here's Perry's."

She watched this minister launch into his ministry under Automotive's roof. He appeared to enlarge, take up space, grow confident. His words were sure, his body language spoke volumes. He didn't once fold his arms across his chest.

Were the young men holy rollers, or merely up for anything that would take them out of the repair pit? Perry himself was an older man, with shoe-polish black hair, receding like Herron's, and thinning. Jimmy and Steve and Malcolm and Ted, all a generation younger, in the usual greasemonkey coveralls with sleeves rolled up to their elbows, on what was turning out to be a fine Indian summer day.

Pauline, with carburetor dust at the back of her throat, was nearly happy to be in Kansas.

In addition to her stuck dilemma (for which they arranged an immediate tow), Herron was working the room for the "Get Focused!" night at St. Alban's, 7:30 to 9:30 this upcoming Wednesday. The station guys made a fuss over Pendleton. The dog ended up with a chew toy in his teeth.

Herron placed a hand on Ted's arm. "I know you'll get something out of this if you give it a chance. One night?" He wore hope in his round, beaming face. Ted and his intentions remained inscrutable.

Pauline whispered to Malcolm, Perry's son, who stood nearest her, a boy of maybe seventeen who wore his hair slicked back, "What day of the week is this?"

"Sunday," he said, with cigarette breath. "Herr's nights at the church are good ones. And we go for beers after."

"Beer's always a plus," Pauline said.

"Wednesday's program," Herron said, handing out his flyers, "will knock your boots off. It's not about belief or unbelief. We won't even talk Bible. I mean, direction of your life, you know? What are your goals? How can we get you there? Positive affirmation and real steps to achieving what you want out of life. It's free. Only two hours. You guys'll come? And we'll cap the night at the Bier House. My treat."

Herron drew her aside. He'd grown sweaty, his eyes shiny. "You'll need to spend the night here, maybe two or three. Perry says the problem might be the solenoid, might be the ignition. Either way, they'll have to send off for parts. Not as bad as it used to be now with the internet, but still, you have to wait for the gosh darn part to arrive, right?"

Pauline shrugged. "Sure, so—"

"So, there's this nice older couple you can stay with while you wait, right next door to me and St. Alban's. That is, if it's okay?" He looked apologetic. "I already called them to feel them out about it. I hope you don't mind. I'm sensing you need some care taking, Pauline. And I'm not trying to insult you, it's just something I'm picking up on. Blame it on me and my line of work. But the Moerleins say it's fine if you bunk with them."

"Better than fine." She didn't even have to think about it. "I can't wait to meet them."

"Johanna and Clem Moerlein. You'll love them, I promise. And they'll love you right back. Kind people, like you, Pauline. And while you're here, we can run some." Herron seemed overall delighted at how Pauline plopped into his Pitiful.

She wondered what kind of pheromones she put out there to make him think her so stable and good. But then she didn't much care, because she was safe and taken in. She hadn't had to call Tom. And Jared still lurked out there, a gold beacon drawing her west, just like that big bridge over the Bay, a prize to work toward once Perry gained the pieces to bring her Bonneville back up to speed.

She turned to Herron. "They won't mind the dog?"

He said, "They'll *love* the dog. They got a crew of their own. What's one more?" He set his arm around her and said, "Girl, let's find you a phone all your own."

Where He Woke

Among unfamiliar surroundings, in a strange apartment, with a mouth of cotton, head full of anvils striking, Jared managed half-mast eyelids, and groaned.

He submerged his consciousness in memories of the way under his hands Pauline whimpered. He spent a lot of time dreaming her. Jared slept naked. He'd slept naked all his life, the way he came into the world, with nothing but what went on in his head and his autonomic nervous system. He slept naked on some girl's couch.

He would have patience, learn patience, know patience, be patience. Patience imagined as a stone slab, and he was that stone, impassive, rigid, patient for the ivy that would clot over the engraving of his name.

His heart pinched as he wondered, had the best with Pauline already fired and fizzled?

He was not prepared to believe this, or even dream this. "So, with us, you and me, you were lying?" he said.

"No, just now I want this other more."

"What is it you have or want, Pauline?"

"Me and my name at the head of every page. I don't want to be the second chapter."

"Did I make you feel that?"

"Mmm, maybe not on purpose. But there's Sten. He never leaves. Never leaves you."

Jared was strewn out like a captive on a street, to be viewed, bones for picking, talked about and laughed at, called fool.

"I love you," he said.

"Ha!" She could not have sounded more bitter, even for a dream girl.

"It's not a line I'm just tossing off. My love for you, Pauline, is the element carving me."

"Carved, yes, that's a good word, but not to describe you. Me. The knife's in your grip. You've always held the knife."

"Good is all I ever aimed to give you," Jared said.

She sucked in a big stuttery breath and shook her head against what he wanted her to be for him. "You're damaged and now you've brought damage to me."

He looked at her, incredulous. "Am I? Have I?"

He took her arm, turned her so she couldn't hide her expression in the couch cushion. What he saw there flattened his hope. She leaned into him with tears marking her face and then bleeding into his shirt. But his chest was bare.

They cried at each other and with each other and for each other. She tore at his clothes, though he was naked, and he tore at hers, but she wore none. They were at each other's mercy and lacking wardrobes.

It was the damnedest dream ever.

Then he smelled toast, burning in his everywhere.

The woman, the barmaid from downstairs, Stacy? Stella? Sandy. Sandy had coffee going, God bless her. And she'd kept the blinds drawn. She padded around barefoot to less disturb. She crunched her toast quietly. All of which Jared appreciated. He lay on Sandy's couch and accepted waking. Sometime in the night she must have covered him with an afghan, soft and fuzzy, hand-knit and much-washed, or much-used. Anyway, it was nice.

He scratched crust from the edges of his eyes, could see her standing at the kitchen counter. She didn't have a table or chairs. She didn't really have a kitchen. It was an eat-in kitchen only if you stood there like Sandy, eating in it. Could have been an eat-in living room, and an eat-in bedroom, and an eat-in bath. Which reminded Jared he had to piss mightily.

"Um," he said rising, with the afghan draped and dragged around his ass. "I'm going down the hall a bit?"

He said it like a question. She gave him a scoot-scoot motion with the hand that did not hold bread.

Her eyes floated above dark circles, the bruised kind, not from abuse but from a metabolism that burned up her body, that kept her looking sleep-deprived. Hair up high in a ponytail, and her face all sleepy-looking, she could have been a teenager, except for the dye job and the dark roots. Or maybe a punk chick, the ones that grew their hair that way purposely. Another woman with attitude – just what he needed. Jared thought all this while he directed his stream into the toilet. He'd sure like some breakfast.

"I need to get to the bank before too long," she said when he came out.

"Got any eggs?"

"Bread, butter, and jam. And the coffee."

"Coffee's good," he said, while she stood counter side and he bent in front of the couch sweep-searching the floor for his jeans. Once tucked inside denim he felt better about facing her, left the afghan go.

She gave him a full mug.

"Thank you kindly, ma'am." He poured it on thick the way he knew women might like if they were in the mood for liking.

He'd always been an easy mark (Sten would say "sucker") for a needy woman, all the way back to that Marnie-Debra duo. He'd like to trip time and tell those girls what he'd really felt over their meanness and conniving, to flip the calendar, withdraw the knife before he ever pulled it on the Tattoo Guy in the DairyMart, to even rail at Sten: No, don't go. Reconsider.

Jared wasn't quite sure what circumstances and the women he'd loved owed him, but he did feel accounts in God's great ledger needed evening up. Pauline was on her way toward him; he tasted her on the wind. She was his payback. He dipped his head to God for looking on him so kindly. He sucked up his coffee, the aroma, the deep color, the heat coming off it.

"I said the bank," Sandy reminded.

He saw she was dressed for errands, not bartending. Big difference. He said, "So go."

"You'll be out of here too, then."

"Sure." He slurped back the rest of the brew, his gut wrangling with it and calling for more substantial input. "Give me a minute to get my boots on."

He followed her out the door and down the steps, said to her back, "Coffee was good. And thanks for the place to crash."

She paused a step or two from the ground; he saw every line etched early around her eyes when she turned to him, the parenthesis mouth from over-grimacing to customers, hustling tips. "You'll be on your way?" she said.

"Yeah, I think so."

She nodded and pivoted in the same motion. He bet she'd practiced the couldn't-give-a-damn shoulder plenty. He wanted to hug her at least but held off until the impulse disintegrated.

The Pontiac smelled swampy with overnight that had settled in through the windows Sandy had only almost closed. He didn't blame her. Nothing but thankfulness spread through him as he sat behind the wheel once more humming west. He had one last quart of oil rolling around in the trunk. He'd need to invest in a few more. The gasket seal must have further rotted.

In driving, he believed he was leaving the worst leaking behind. In California, he'd begin over and if he dreamed her hard enough, Pauline would appear. He was kind of hung up on the way things were meant to be and trusting fate and all that rot. "Refer to the gasket seal, and learn, little brother," Sten said, but Jared was too inside his hope and his hangover to heed ghost caution. And he just wouldn't think about what his fleeing Illinois meant in the eyes of the court.

One minute he rimmed the far side of Reno, then he blinked his eyes open on a lovely little California town called Truckee, toward Tahoe.

Cruising through all the state's beauties to the ocean was his intent, but the Pontiac begged minding. Long before Sacramento, Jared pulled into another of the half-dozen or more mom-and-pop joints he'd lit into for cigarettes and snacks, for gasoline and drink and replacement oil, or to piss.

He strode into Marlon's Kash 'em, which proudly accepted "only American hand-in-the-palm currency for your purchase." Jared wondered if this was survivalist country, where men buried ammunitions on their properties, anticipating the clash with their own government, but he shook free of that.

Three hunting buddies – or maybe not hunting, maybe camo was what they always dressed in – mulled around the canned foods, gathering to their chests tins of pork and beans and SpaghettiOs and Vienna sausage. Things you could eat cold in case you had no heat, or preferred no fire.

Others trawled the place, a woman among them. Always a woman, right? Her presence at his elbow threw him off balance. He meant to proceed paying for Gatorade, smokes, the Valvoline, and the unleaded he'd already pumped outside, but she smelled like a rodeo, the good horsey smell both girls and boys fell in love with on their first pony rides. In jeans and buffalo plaid flannel, she dressed like Pauline, not fancied up but easy with how her clothes touched her body, implying she'd be easy with you touching her, too.

She stood on tiptoes to peek over his shoulder. "You like the orange?" she said.

Jared thrilled to her tap, even more to her twang. He said, "Lemon-lime chokes me."

"Sounds like you need honeyed tea more than any sports drink."

He cleared his throat. "I just ain't spoke in a while."

"Traveling alone, are you?"

"I am."

"You like that solitude?"

"Mostly."

"You don't find it lonesome?"

He shrugged. "Now and then. Gives me time to think, though."

"Something specific you're thinking about?"

He couldn't help smiling, and when the smile took hold

he felt he hadn't used those muscles in ages. "You're awful curious about me, a stranger, aren't you?"

"Just making conversation 'til I settle up." She held a package of Lorna Doones and linked cans of root beer.

"I see you're going nutritious, too," he said.

She lifted the six-pack. "I'm laying off the alcohol." She paused, then broke into the world's flashiest grin. "At least until sundown."

She had teeth white as snow caps – horsey teeth – another reason she blinded him, a good blinding.

Jared paid, pocketed his wallet, lifted his three saggy plastic bags. "Well, watch the sugar, sugar," he said. He winked at her as he scooted his stuff aside for hers. She returned the wink, and her accompanying smile made him tarry.

He remembered sugar cubes, sticky in his cupped boy-hand, held to ponies at the edge of a fence, enticing them to jump. At that time he believed animals, or anything, anyone, could be trained to do what he wanted. He'd read about Pavlov and the dog. He wanted the horse to leap; even some salivating through those rubbery Mr. Ed lips would prove he, Jared, commanded. He saw he'd been angling for Pauline to drool over him.

Marlon rang up the woman's sweet-tooth indulgences. She met Jared, still struggling at the door. He was lingering. He had two things at once going in his head: Pauline of before, and this girl.

A weather-worn picnic table had been set on bare ground behind Marlon's, sheltered by giant trees and their limbs. Now that he'd crossed into California, everything appeared gargantuan – trees, lakes, light, what he touched on, what bled from his touch. Something was about to spill out of him, and he didn't know what it was going to be, but he felt it condensing like a storm out over water.

"Care to sit?" he said to her.

Their bags rustled as they planted themselves under the trees. He endured the memory of sitting with Marnie at the picnic table behind Deb's house years ago. Funny, what would precipitate thoughts like that to cruise through?

"If you don't mind, I'll stand," he said. "Been sitting way too much."

"Sure," she said, all accommodating, all teeth, all sugar.

"Jared," he said.

"I'm Bess."

They shook hands. Introductions at this point seemed really funny to them both so they laughed. She tore open the cookies she'd bought and offered him the package. He dove in.

"So you're from?" she said.

"The meandering Midwest," he said around his working mouth.

"And here because?"

"Because it's on the way."

"To?"

"California."

"You're there," she said. "Or here."

"Yes. But further."

"Ah." She nodded and squinted as if she were sizing him up by his travel choices. "The ocean. Everybody's headed to the coast."

"If only to see it." He hadn't managed yet to put into words what he'd set off seeking.

"So you'll see it, and then?"

He smiled and shrugged. "Won't know what's next 'til I feel the sand shift under me."

"Well, I hope it kicks start something for you," she said.

"Mountains are more to my liking. Ravines, rocky cliffs and dense woods you can lose yourself in."

Losing himself would feel good right about now, Jared reasoned. He recalled Sandy and the night before, and acknowledged, sadly, there was no losing himself in any other woman but Pauline. She'd marked him; he wore her groove.

But still.

Here sat lovely Bess, within his grasp, he was sure, if he wished. And he thought maybe he did. He could feel the much-washed flannel of her shirt, and her substantial form beneath it. All he had to do was reach.

Shit, she was encouraging him, with her wide-set eyes as open as the sea he'd been moving toward for three days, and something tricky behind them, waiting to link him, the two of them tangled like office drawer paper clips.

"You're a hiker?" he said.

"I've done on trail and off. Prefer the uncharted. More adventure."

"I don't have the right footwear, I don't think."

"You can start out easy. No sense investing in extras when you don't know how far you're gonna go."

"You know some trails around here?"

"Lived here all my life," she said. "I doubt there's a trail I haven't walked."

He crossed to her side of the table, brushed cookie crumbs from the front of her shirt. She'd been nibbling like a mouse with those big teeth of hers. "You're making a bit of a mess," he said.

She shrugged. "I've been known to."

He felt her shoulders slight as bird bones when he sat and put his arm around her before the kiss. She leaned into him and left free whatever tension she'd been holding since inside Marlon's, even her mouth collapsed into his. She tasted the way he imagined a cookie factory's air tasted, with no room for any other senses to horn in. He hadn't realized how hungry he was.

And he didn't know why she was so open. He should have wondered more about that.

The hunters were on him before he knew it, hemming him, dragging him from the girl's kiss, Jared fumbling to gather his goods up off the table. Its splintery surface stabbed him. He was going to need a needle.

He was a student of *déjà vu* and dreams and repeating the past, the doom of his own stupidity swinging round and bashing him in the head. As a boy, he'd had plenty of practice separating himself from pain. He lay beat-up in the parking lot of a roadside convenience store, with the law moving in.

Maybe if Sten had real armor or Kevlar like the vests those hunter guys wore, or whatever the hell they passed out to the guys on the ground, he'd have survived. Maybe Sten survived still.

No one knew. No body had been recovered.

Jared resisted the vision of his brother blown to bits by a roadside bomb or a firefight that incinerated the few things that still moved and grew in Afghanistan. All the poppy fields, they came through it, didn't they? They were goddamned protected, by both sides. Sten's life wasn't worth one plot of poppies? These were Jared's thoughts as he heard the siren wail then quit loud in his bashed-to-shit ear.

A state trooper held up a baton as he moved in to examine Jared. "Feels particular cumbersome on the throat, so don't make me use it."

"No, sir." He thought it; did he say it?

"ID?"

That took a while to locate. The camo guys, perhaps in cahoots with Bess, had gone through Jared's wallet and stole everything but his license, which the law plucked. While he lay back on the ground, he heard the dispatcher and the disembodied voices trading his facts and figures. Him and his car were all he had.

Everything relied on the past, didn't it? Not like he was wanted for embezzlement or murder or insider trading – all equal evils in Jared's view. He pulled a knife once on a guy, but he didn't use it. He might have threatened. Threat was all in the eyes and the tilt of the arm, that old *en garde* stance.

His viewpoint, that had been churning western dust, stalled in the back of the state trooper's vehicle. He had a wrenched neck because of those guys who'd fled, like the girl, and no witnesses. Marlon, especially, didn't know nothing, he said.

Jared, as the stranger to these parts, appeared the interloper. And wanted in Illinois for shucking his probation.

"Boy, I don't need to mess with you," the trooper said, spiffed and inscrutable behind the cliché shades of every Bandit movie sheriff. "You're going back east all 'cause of your own screwed business."

The legalities twisted Jared's neck one more knob, reversing his California direction. He heard a pop, or maybe the simple gunshot, of every bird hunt and manhunt he and Sten had ever conducted.

At the time of his breakdown in college they'd recommended therapy, said he held things inside him 'til he blew. Blew a gasket just like the Pontiac, Sten laughed.

"My car?" Jared said. He talked around a few loose

teeth.

"Oh, we'll save it for you," the trooper said. "We'll impound it; how's that?"

"I own—" Jared swallowed some blood and restarted. "I own it free and clear."

"I'm not arguing there. Nobody'll get it but you."

Jared felt like narrowing his eyes but found he was already squinting through a swollen view.

"We just need to get you looked at right now. Your precious Pontiac's parked."

"The fuckers—"

The baton dug his beat-up ribs.

"Hey! No call for that talk. Ain't a soul here but Marlon, who, if you'd like to know, called me to your sweet aid."

Marlon, law-abiding citizen, good Samaritan, probably in on the coup from the get-go. Jared's bones screamed weary. His mouth sat salted with his own blood, and swollen with the cuts inside there. His head ached from the pummeling he must have taken but, damn, he didn't even recall the fight.

He fled himself, or burrowed deeper inside, a defense he acknowledged his dear mama and others had instilled and nurtured. He had ribs front and back either cracked or bruised or both.

The trooper's car could be his sleep haven, but Jared vowed not to nod off. He had to be sharp. What was that quote about a stranger in a strange land? Was it Jesus? Or some French writer? Nothing stranger than California. He dared not even blink.

"You might as well relax, son. You're seeing no one but the doc." The trooper's knuckle-knock against the roof of the car reverberated in Jared's temples and his jaw and the roots of his wobbly teeth.

Then they flew down the highway to an antiseptic room for care.

Not the first time he'd been left with nothing. Consider why he lit out from Pittsburgh: Sten's enlistment, and in his absence little else. All across the Midwest Jared scoured the ground for something that would sustain him, just like those mongrel bastards with the canned goods who'd busted his head and kidneys.

He'd found focus in Euphoria. He'd found focus in Pauline, he'd thought. And then he flew and blamed the flight on her.

Now there'd be no San Fran, no water, no coastal light, no sea air future. After a patch-up in the closest ER, he'd be traveling the way he'd just come, eyes locked on the Mississippi. The one thing that soothed him in his down-and-out capture: they'd be boosting him back to Pauline.

His out-loud laugh had his captor eying him in the driver's rearview.

The likelihood of uniting with Pauline *was* laughable when he examined the odds, but Jared had lived with the negative slant all his life. He knew he had some reconciling up his road, tried envisioning what his return would really mean. Capitulation, relinquishing a dream, and letting go any hope of Sten.

Sten. Might as well admit it: hadn't this cross-country flight been less about brother and more about lover? Jared's greatest con was ever of himself. He'd left on account of Pauline, as a means of acquiring Pauline, to entice Pauline, offering her the chance to prove herself. And why did he do that? He needed proof?

Fuck that excuse. He was already as sure as any man could be of a woman. He might simply be a coward. He was a boy who hated sighting doves down the barrel of a gun, watching them explode in the sky above him, dodging the blood and guts he expected that never fell because there was nothing left of them to rain.

They, like Sten, had simply vanished.

What did Sten say back in that field of stubble the time they'd first hunted when they failed to find the one bird Jared had managed to shoot? His brother's smudged-ugly face taunting him, "What you're looking for you can't find. Better get used to it, bro."

Was there anything worse than being browbeaten by a ghost?

You are the needle in the groove of a broken record. The song's always a woman, with you flailing around, latching on to one or the other blonde's arm, hopeful for deliverance or redemption or a sign you're worth anybody's sacrifice.

Jared said, "Women and roads are all the same."

The state trooper said, "What's that?" No turn or check in the mirror or easing up his lead foot.

Swelling prevented Jared from twisting his lips in a sneer at his driver and all the ignoramuses he'd bounced off, from Pittsburgh to Evansville, Euphoria to Gloria, and even this lauded west, where he'd imagined light would shine differently. But he'd have to be different, too, and he wasn't.

He was ever and only a boy injured within when he shot at a dove. He was boy and bird, both dropped out of the sky and standing still, watching himself plummet.

Talk to Me

Pauline's heart hammered. Her eyes adjusted while furniture formed into a sit-before dresser, its mirror reflecting an off-kilter window sash and closet and her stripped, road-grimy clothes. She was marooned in Pitiful. She'd slept deep and dreamless in the Moerlein's daughters' old room, upon meeting the Moerleins and accepting their invitation, following Father Herron Gallagher's Sunday night service at St. Alban's while her Bonneville had its guts exposed at Perry's Automotive.

The dogs Sadie and Flynn soaked up the love Johanna and Clem once lavished on now-grown, gone children. The linens, the drapes, the wall colors of this place: no-nonsense gray and sepia, barnyard brown and white. The whole scene was very nearly Amish to Pauline, with its Spartan cleanliness and lack of fuss.

As were her hosts, dressed as they'd been in sensible church outfits. Clem wore a string tie. In case Pauline forgot she'd arrived in the American West, this reminded her. A shirtwaist dressed Johanna's gaunt frame. Her posture suggested she suffered back pain. Or maybe she curled to Clem that way out of devotion.

They were side-by-side trees with grown-together roots. Pauline gathered they'd frown on waste and expense and uncalled-for attention, and while in their house she pledged to eat her every toast crust.

The idea of bread brought up some curdled belly business. Pauline vaulted to sitting, and grabbed under the bed for her shoes. The hallway tilted, or she did. Touching the wall to steady, she felt perspiration rise along her skin.

Clem was peering into the medicine chest mirror, shaving before the sink in the open bathroom, but he methodically set the razor on top of the toilet tank and didn't catch her in time.

She found herself on the couch with ice on her head and her hands stacked in Johanna's, Johanna slapping them.

"You had us worried." The sweat of Johanna's hands and hairline telegraphed a woman full of bustle, and Pauline had interrupted her purposeful flow. Because of Pauline, something was not cooking, not baking, not being sponged.

Clem and Herron leaned their concern over the sofa back like Tin Man and Scarecrow, with Johanna acting as Pauline's very own Auntie Em. A warmth spread through her, which she enjoyed until she thought maybe she'd peed the couch, and, mortified, she tried standing.

The Kansas folk hemmed her in, insisted she sit, she stay. Like one of their dogs receiving orders – the dogs they loved, so they were loving orders, but orders still – she acquiesced. Outside the house, Pendleton barked and romped with Sadie and Flynn, having himself a ball. She patted the ice pack on her head.

"Did I hurt myself?"

"Did you?" said Herron. His blue eyes were almost merry. What did he have to be so happy about?

"You were out cold," Clem said. He was a man who wore overalls. Rare to find overalls at the Goodwill, Pauline realized, because men like Clem wore them to rags.

"You hit the deck," he said. "Like a sack of potatoes, you dropped."

Johanna said, "Sounded like a crash. Like the time we had that earthquake, remember, Clem? We never have earthquakes, but we had that one. When the breakfront pitched forward? Remember? That mess of the dishes." She turned to Pauline. "You've been ill?"

"No." Pauline saw Herron's eyes shift. On the ride to last night's service, she'd shared with him the basics of her California destination and her tangle of two men. But that was lovesickness. This felt different, body-based.

"Well, I was queasy yesterday when I got up, but … I've been traveling, and the diet's probably suffered."

"You should stop and sit down for a good meal," Johanna said. "Give your whole constitution a break. Let things digest in the way they need. The road will always be there."

"I do wolf it down," Pauline said. She acknowledged for them what she'd weathered of late – the stress, and the travel and the drinking and crummy food when she bothered to eat. Her constant ache over Jared she kept secret.

Clem clapped his hands together. "How about Mother here scrambles us some eggs—"

Pauline's hand covered a noxious burp. "Oh, I couldn't—"

Herron skirted the sofa, bent and embraced her shoulder, tucked her within his shower-fresh protection. Clem and Johanna were dears the way they brimmed with vigilance.

"I've got fresh cornbread," Johanna said.

Pauline saw they'd not let her loose until she put something in her mouth.

"I could maybe manage that, with some milk and coffee."

Clem said, "We've always got coffee, don't we, Mother?"

Pauline smiled. "Just let me get decent before I join you at the table?"

Clem and Johanna looked away politely from her high-thigh jersey gym shorts and her baby doll pajama top, where her left breast slid half-free of the bra part.

Herron said, "I'll take you back. Lean on me while we walk." He helped her to her feet, testing her rolling insteps, her noodly lower limbs.

"When did we board ship?" she said, making fun with him down the hallway. "Next you'll have me walking the plank." She took a deep breath in and then blew it out. "I guess I'm one who gets seasick."

"Arrrgh," he said into her neck, pretending to bite.

"There are spiders in my room," she whispered.

Interrupting his pirate act, Herron said, "Over-wintering."

"Huh?"

"Come fall, spiders search for a warm place inside."

"So they choose my room?"

He spread his arm through her open door. "Live and let live, all will be fine."

She said, "If I see one, I'm stepping on it."

Pauline spent a day and night in bed, Herron's fingers drumming her back, him droning about concussion, being watchful, replenishing and readjusting her ice, each time dragging her up to consciousness.

She scatter-dreamed of the news sheet in purple type, *The Watch Tower,* that Jehovah Witnesses pushed on you at the door if you were foolish enough to answer their testifying. When someone's trying to convince you to change your life you need more than shocking color and volume. A tequila worm in your heart would be a start. Worms and spiders and crickets.

She dreamed she pawned the pearls to pay for her car repair. At the counter in Ken's Keep, a shutter-darkened shop that didn't exist beyond dreams, a bald man with a gut-busted shirt paid her ten one-hundred dollar bills.

"What he gave me was genuine," she said, speaking of the pearls not the money, to Pendleton who stood beside her on his hind legs like a cartoon animal.

"The wanting reshaped me, made me a skinnier, starved lover," she said.

Fat-man Ken polished his forehead with a dark blue handkerchief, which might have been velvet. Then he moved on to buffing the pearls.

From the curtained employee area at the back of the shop, she heard Tom say, "Talk to me, and I'll talk back."

She fled then, tight-fisting the money. The dog, once again on all four limbs, bounded after her onto a street in a deserted Western town.

She opened her eyes many times, found Herron sitting there, and quick closed them so she wouldn't have to talk. She didn't want him interpreting her dreams.

Yesterday's same light drew the room out of its gloom; the furniture appeared where it was. She wore her same bedclothes on her stale-smelling body. Herron had vanished, and she breathed deeply. She did not like being observed. She heard crickets chirping from the window well.

Sitting up turned her shaky. She reached for her shoes under the bed, scattering the spiders. In the free bathroom, she threw up in the toilet and felt immediately improved. A hot shower, clean clothes, teeth and tongue scrubbed – all made her better, or appear better.

Johanna had the kitchen table covered with ingredients and implements for what looked like Baking Day. In Pauline's childhood back in Euphoria, Monday had always been Cleaning Day, and she the official duster.

She resisted casting back to that time. Thinking of her passed-on mother could stall her in her tracks. Estranged during the years Pauline traveled the road with Neal, and then her mom's massive coronary prevented the opportunity to reconcile. Pauline shook her shoulders, shivered away her mother-memories.

Up to her elbows in flour, Johanna nodded toward the coffee pot, and as Pauline poured, she said, "Come here. I want to show you something."

Pauline had made cobbler and crumbles, but Johanna was about to divulge the secret of perfect pie crust. She supposed the polite thing to do was pretend attention. As long as the coffee remained within reach she thought she could. She would do it as part of honoring her mom.

"Flaky, light, short – you want all those things," Teacher said. "And when you are ready, you bow your head."

Pauline said, "You pray over the pie dough?" She touched the knot on the back of her skull.

"Well, some folks think of it as prayer. We'll call it, for now, holding good intent in your heart while you're kneading and rolling it."

Then Johanna drew herself tall as her apron and her spinal stenosis would allow. "Yes, pray, damnit. What's so wrong with prayer? Or admitting it guides your life just as much as those stars up above? Hmm?"

How the woman reminded Pauline of Maudie right then. She bet no one had been by to visit her or Hollis since she started her quest. She should call Fiona – no, she should call Tom and urge him to check in on the old folks. They were her only family.

"We're smart people, intelligent beings," Pauline said. "Shouldn't we—" And here she twirled her hand until she recognized the Tom-motion she usually mocked, and she quit.

"Shouldn't we know more? About what we want? Shouldn't it be easier somehow? I mean life."

"Maybe we would, but then there's this," Johanna said. She pointed the big wooden stirring spoon at her breastbone. "And," she added, "desire."

"Yeah. I probably need to shed free of all that."

Johanna's eyes flickered over Pauline head to toe. "Whatever for?" she said. "Desire's God's main course."

Pauline hoped, had her mom lived, they might have met like this in talk over a table.

"I need some stability," Pauline said. She worked a tiny bit of dough back and forth hand to hand. Then she popped it into her mouth and chewed it, with a flash memory of her mother cautioning, Raw dough will give you worms. Her belly soured and resurrected the idea of the tequila worm from her dream.

"Work at the Dollar Tree," Johanna said. "Those register lines move so slow they need a smart girl like you."

Pauline hadn't been called a girl since, since Jared. His dreaminess had first drawn her and she wanted him dreamy, but she wanted him accountable, too.

"Oh, I'm not staying here," Pauline said.

"Aren't you?" Johanna, with her head tilted, watched Pauline as her hands worked the crust.

"I didn't mean so much stability of place as ..." and here Pauline drifted. She liked Johanna and admired the life she'd created, but this woman was not her mother and she was no girlfriend and she was not Jared, and Jared was where Pauline planned confessing all.

With the pie in the oven, they poured second cups of coffee and Johanna sat with her.

They sipped and listened to the crickets.

Johanna smiled. "Noisy little critters."

Pauline said, "They're nice."

"You know what crickets' constant chirping means?"

"Hmm. What?"

"Well, countries' folklores interpret different ways. But one ... money's expected."

"Oh yeah? Great. I'm ready for a big payday." One thousand dollars, she recalled, for her dream pearls. "What else do crickets say?" She held her palms open as if she expected them read.

Johanna placed one hand in Pauline's and twirled her spoon on the table with the other. She started to speak, but then the spoon flipped free and hit the floor. Once retrieved, she sat straight as she could and said, "How're you feeling today?"

Pauline's hands were back folded in her lap. She nodded. "Good, good." She was distracted by a dream of money.

"The bump?"

"Not a bother."

"Herron watched out for you all day and half the night," Johanna said.

"That I did," Herron said. There he was, face pressed to the kitchen screen door.

Johanna motioned him inside even as he was entering.

Pauline said, dramatically, "My hero, my Herron."

"You better believe it," he said.

Nervy, Pauline thought.

"Are you up for a run?"

"Herron, she just suffered a concussion."

"No. I didn't. I mean, not a concussion, and yeah, I'd love to run. My head is fine." She emphasized to Johanna, "Fine."

Clem said, "What's going on here?" He'd entered and turned on the faucet, rubbed soap suds into his palms and his fingernails.

Johanna winked. "They're going running."

"Used to be," Clem said, "if a woman was running, it was either from trouble or she was rushing to tear clothes off the line before it rained."

Pauline had the horrid idea that Johanna was matchmaking.

Outside she and Herron began a slow jog and Herron said, "We'll keep it easy like this. I don't want to work you hard. You're in recovery."

She would not debate her health with him, nor what she was and was not fit for. Once they were well away from the house, she spotlighted him when she said, "They don't know you're gay?"

Maintaining his pace forced his smile into a weird almost-leer.

He said, "Points for smarts there, Pauline. And extra credit for not mentioning it before now. Clem probably has some idea. Johanna … she sees what she wants to see."

"Well, your eye for guys is good news for me, dear

minister. Because if I have one more man circling, my light's going to burn out, I swear."

"Nah, Pauline. Your light's never going to go out."

She puffed air through her mouth, and sweat and spit both flew. And her half contempt.

"Honest, Pauline. You've got the kind of light can't ever fade."

"What's this? Affirmation garbage you work into your sermons?"

"From what I've observed, it hasn't hurt anybody yet. Seriously. In my line of work, what I've surmised, Pauline … we don't love ourselves well enough. None of us."

A crew was remodeling a house two blocks from St. Alban's, along the route Herron led her. She supposed he ran this way every day, probably showing off his legs to the hard hats.

"Looking good," she called to the workers, to rise above her feet pounding and her pulse pounding. When was running supposed to get easier?

"Building it from the inside out," one worker said.

Pauline yelled, jogging backward but slow, keeping her elbows lifted, "Good bones on the old girl, yeah?"

"Good innards," a guy, nodding up on the roof, agreed.

Jared had said, "You've got good bones, Pauline," touching her face as he said so. "Cheekbones, all-over lovely bones. I'd bet my world on the strength of your backbone, girl."

"Hey, come on," Herron teased. He had half a block on her.

Catching up made her head thud, but she didn't care.

"Your legs are prettier than mine," she laughed, pointing as they jogged together.

He shook his head, denying and blushing. They looked

ahead of them to the road and then stole looks at each other, thighs to ankles, comparing. Herron's *were* prettier.

"Nah, Pauline. Nah," he said.

They ran silently for a while.

"So how come, if you love this guy, you haven't left him? I mean left your husband."

She wobbled, and wondered if this whole running deal was one way he wormed in his ministering. Her belly started souring again.

"What do you mean? I did leave," she said. "I'm here, not there, right?"

Herron gave her a *come on, truth* look.

She sighed as much as anyone can sigh and keep pace. "What I had with Tom, time and obligation – Tom would say obligation was promise. And water under the bridge that we've survived." Her voice trailed off.

Herron took her hand and they both stopped, breathing hard into each other's face. He said, "That water's so far into the sea, whatever togetherness comprised that water a long time ago fled its currents, apart apart. There was, *there is,* no obligation there, Pauline." Then he said, "Honey, you can't go through this world in a suit of armor."

But that's exactly what she'd been doing, and Jared, too. She couldn't carry him and those two suits of armor any longer. Three suits, because he'd been carrying his brother's, too, with his stubborn hope inside it for Sten. Why wasn't she company enough?

Pauline would give up this road, give it up like she gave up chocolate, meaning not very well, and certainly not forever. The idea of Jared, and loving him, would never vanish, but the notion of linking with him on his trek had been fading, if she were honest with herself, ever since she crossed the Mississippi.

Crazy to think they'd manage to meet, without plan or promise, anywhere within the middle of the wide United States, or even at the edge where cliff plunges into ocean.

At the rectory, she and Herron walked next door, up the driveway.

The Moerleins' dogs, Flynn and Sadie, romped with Pendleton, who had never appeared so joyous to Pauline as he did with those two mutts in the corral Clem had rigged.

"They look happy, yeah?" she said.

"Dogs don't want much."

"Lucky dogs."

Herron said, "What about you, Pauline? What is it you want? Have you asked yourself this?"

"Ha. Yes. All the time. Constantly."

"And?"

"I want to be one man's first thought and his last desire." She couldn't believe she let that pop out. Herron managed to get to her – how did he do that? She struggled to keep her face clear of emotion. She looked up from scratching Pendleton in his scruff. "Is that too much to ask?"

"What of the other two?"

"Tom's first thought is Tom. And Jared's first thought is ... Sten. So you see where I sit."

Herron paused a good minute. They moved to a backyard bench Clem had anchored for Johanna so she could gaze at the field, if the woman ever lingered in place long enough to do that. They sat and stretched their legs out before them. He said, "And, Pauline, if I can ask, what or who is *your* first thought?"

She bent to massage her twitching calf muscle. Her mind remained blank, but at her center, she was agitated. What rang in her ears, along with her slowing pulse was a snip from a song she'd written for Neal: The way you walk on water, baby/makes me wanna swim. Which did not mean Neal was her topmost desire, not at all. This simply revealed how essential her songwriting was to her.

As if he could read her mind, he said, "Try me."

She said, "What's the word from Perry?"

"Like a lawyer or a doctor, what's told to me stays with me," Herron said.

He could knock all he wanted, she wasn't letting him in.

"Do you think tomorrow I could be on my way?"

"West … or east?"

"Down the road."

Herron said, "That's no answer."

Pauline turned inward, and heard, in her mind, the creek that ran below her property, how its sound lent the idea of movement and purpose and influence and going, a body of water with which she could flow.

She thought she'd been slipping away from her home on the hill, the house she'd gained by her own efforts, no one else's.

She'd supposed the trek would be easy, meant to be, and now, for the first time, she considered going back. The creek swayed with its ways, and was hard at work trying to convince her that change was possible, that new stones could be found and their rough edges smoothed, that a new locale waited where the water intended to flow. It did not stop.

The creek only knew forward, it only knew further. Not like a road. A road could end. A road often ends. A road will end. Two states away, and with her eyes closed, Pauline saw the ocean, the tease of it, as the canyon dropped away.

She said, "I should check in with Tom."

"Call him on your new phone," Herron said.

"I believe I will." She stood, and endured some dizziness.

Herron, still seated, squinted up at her. He said, "You going to tell him?"

"What?

"Pauline," he said. "Two men, for this amount of time? Don't pretend you've got no idea."

She stared at the dogs loping at the edges of their pen. Just animals, the dogs had no answers except eat, shit and sleep.

Pauline said, "Do you hear those crickets?"

She went into the house and shut herself behind the door of the Moerleins' daughters' old room.

In her ear, Tom said, "Where's this number? Where're you calling from?"

She remembered what he said when she left, "Close the door and go." Compared that with Jared, his most familiar geography, every rise and valley of him.

She shut down the phone's radioactive glow.

Outside, Johanna rapped her knuckles on the door jamb. She said, "Hon, you all right in there?"

"Yes," Pauline said. Sweat dripped and nausea rose. "Yes," she said again, louder, bringing her forearm to her face.

She watched baby spiders clinging to the hem of the bedspread while they lifted one or two legs. Pauline felt wobbly, felt the cyclone about to rush her.

Ferried Back

About nine days since Jared had last seen Pauline and he thought, in a pinch, he could feed off memories. He looked out of the window, fourteen thousand feet above the American West, at the scarred, variable planet. Depression colored him, just a little. If you were being escorted by a U.S. Marshall you, too, might not skim the emotional heights. His hands cuffed in his lap prevented most every act – unlatching his tray table, releasing his seatbelt, reclining. If he tried, he might, but he refrained. He wanted to see what he could live without, since his foreseeable future would be steeped in denial.

They rode on an MD-90, with two seats to the left, a skinny aisle, then a trio of seats right. The Marshall had secured first row in cabin class so passengers would be less likely to spy him and freak about traveling alongside a prisoner.

Jared sat in the middle of three, cramped in on himself, while his federal escort stretched his legs in the walkway. Jared's lost brother Sten soaked up the window view.

Yes, Sten, wearing full camo and his face muddy-bloodied as if he'd just quit rousting the Afghan hovels for

Bin Laden, said, "Do not let the woman fuck with your head. Man, look at you running on what roils below your gut. What were you thinking?"

"Putting it to her."

"To what? Try and force her hand?"

"Asking her to own what she felt."

"You're gonna ruin her life. If you haven't already."

"Because I ruin everything?" he said to Sten. Squinting helped him endure the cerebral fog and ache from being pummeled at the highway rest stop. Two teeth busted in the mugging were in need of root canals right after he processed at the Lincoln County jail. Currently, the pieces left in his gums thumped and drummed.

"No," his brother said, "because it all goes to ruin. Love has to implode, rule of physics. It's a flock eating away at the sky."

Sten had not been so poetic in real life. Jared's wish for guidance fashioned his brother into a goddamn sensei.

Sten said, "About time you quit this woman, ain't it?"

Jared stiffened in his cramped seat. Quitting Pauline could not be done.

"Maybe it's time I'm done with *you,*" Jared said. His gums supported their own heartbeat.

The plane hit turbulence, dipped down and leveled. Sten's edges began flickering like the map of California set afire in the opening to *Bonanza.* He burned away in Jared's brain, curling in, off, and to nothing until that pith and pity of a brother propped up and idolized for so long, he melted, too. And then no more Sten.

The Marshall poked a finger in Jared's side. "You need a pain pill, son?"

Men calling him *son* is what half-landed Jared in this situation. It got his back up. No one around he could have called *father*, so none around with the right to call him *son.* He relaxed the grimace he'd felt masking his face, opened his eyes to a plane flooded with light from across-the-aisle windows.

"Banking," the Marshall said, ducking the sun.

Jared said, "What I crave is a cigarette." He extended his linked together hands.

"No sin in that," the Marshall said.

The pilot breathed into the intercom, "We've been cleared for our approach."

The flight attendants enforced landing rules, secured the passengers, and scurried through their last trash collection. Jared dry swallowed drugs the Marshall parceled out. He was alone in weathering pain, his Crutch Brother all burned up. He felt the gamut of his thump-fucking head, every cling-clang in his skull, and especially the echo when they hit the tarmac.

He thanked the doctors they'd left in the State of California for Vicodin that smoothed his crash-down into Euphoria.

Because of the absconding, his assault and battery soft-pedaled by probation and community service rose up into a dragon that bit him in the ass.

"Leave the state and you leave yourself wide open to it, son," the judge said. Gavel down.

Jared and his case shuffled, a dumb animal in procession. In booking, he stripped down to his socks – funny, they let him try to keep his toes warm in this god-awful chill – and emerged in the jumpsuit attire you see guys collecting highway trash wearing. He could only presume the greasy feel of the walls as he walked the corridors to his cell.

Sensations hovered at arm's length, and maybe would as long as jail time ruled. He could not think what had landed him here, the events and the stupid act of leaving Illinois to force his woman's hand. And where was she now?

All-dream-Pauline took backseat to the five cellmates who watched his entrance with little pity and less enthusiasm. He wobbled, he with his mattress and the paltry bedding he carried, through the held open bars. A woman guard – "Esther" her stitched-in-shirt name read – escorted him, then locked up behind his shoulder.

Outside, but visible from certain vantage points and from the most prized bunks inside the cell, a color TV bolted to the ceiling ran a *Wheel of Fortune* puzzle. In one corner of the cell there sat a crapper, and above it a steel sink, privacy enabled by an old sheet strung from the ceiling.

Couldn't piss or worse without all knowing, all the cellmates hearing. Next to it a crude shower, a second makeshift stall thanks to a slimy curtain pretending waterproofing that no sane man, given the option, would touch. But sanity had little purchase here.

Final-guy Jared got shafted just as in a children's game where the last to show up got tagged "it." He shoved his mattress into the steel frame of the unclaimed bunk nearest the privy, started to tuck the sheet then lost heart, let it sit anchored by the blanket's puny weight.

That sheet, he would soon discover, might otherwise waft right to the concrete floor from the swirl kicked up by the men ambling around the center picnic table steel-bolted to the floor. From the minute he arrived – and perhaps he'd interrupted their rhythm and that's why they scowled at his entrance – his bunkmates plodded around the sole, immovable piece of furniture. They circled the table, for exercise, bored or antsy, spooked or mentally infirm, maybe to provoke.

Jail was a damned loony bin.

"Custom made for you then, eh, bro?" The visual haunt might have got zapped on the plane ride, but Sten's voice still ghosted through Jared's brain.

"Hey, chipmunk," a graying man of lanky build and lankier hair said.

"Got a mouth full of grapes?" That from a yellow-headed, buzz-cut Nazi with tattoos up the back of his bull neck.

"Storing nuts for the winter?" said a tall dude with the shakes. Honest to God, he might have been afflicted with Parkinson's, but disease didn't dilute his meanness. Shakey said, "I got some nuts for you." He grabbed his own crotch.

The usual razz and strut raging in too small a space, residents enforcing the pecking order.

Jared's arrival was their shot in the arm, the blip in their flat line.

"Teeth trouble," he mumbled. He considered extending a hand, then let go that thought. His jaw and gums still fucking alive, swollen, thumping a different beat from the rest of his circulation. He actually looked forward to the root canals scheduled in a day, and more so to his palliative Vicodin.

Following lunch – not that he could eat much – of soggy pot pie, bologna on bread (was that the appetizer?), and limp lettuce, there were Jared's pain meds, and Shakey's meds, dispensed by Esther.

He saw what the guy swallowed, and though he couldn't ID them, the number and size astounded. Enough to tranquilize a buffalo, but Shakey continued vibrating like an earthquake after time elapsed in which drugs might have made a difference.

"Man, what would happen if you didn't get yours?" Jared said.

"You wouldn't want to know," he growled. "Like a car with a blowout, like a car minus steering, like a fish flopping sick 'round the bottom of your boat."

Jared backed up to his bunk and sat his ass down, all the while showing his hands in the signal "no harm."

The gray-haired tall drink of water ambled over and sat on Jared's bunk. His teeth were a brown-out mess. He said, "Drugs barely work for that guy. Thank God for the drugs."

Jared nodded.

A quick flick of his greasy head, then Gray-guy said "I'm Benneteri. What're you here for?"

"Call me Jared. Assault and then absconding."

"Tough. Me? I've got my freakin' old lady claiming domestic violence shit."

"Did you do it?"

The guy, besides his crappy teeth, had one roaming eye, which made looking at him while conversing fucking disconcerting.

A satanic smile crept across Benneteri's lips. "Maybe, maybe not."

This seemed like baiting to Jared. He didn't say a word.

Benneteri kept his backbone straight. He could have had some kind of rod running through him, and Jared saw how this posture imposed advantage.

"Blind fucking drunk," Benneteri said. "We fought, yeah. She left. She says I kicked her in the back when she was sitting on the stoop outside the trailer smoking. 'My kidneys,' she claims. Whatever. I don't remember, but that I'm sure not confessing. She chased me with a skillet earlier, I know that. She's ain't blameless. Me neither, I guess. It all depends on who calls the cops and then who the cops believe."

Jared kept mum, just nodded. He bet he'd be doing a lot of nodding in here. The noncommital nod.

Benneteri said, "You got a woman?"

Jared gave a sly smile. "Shit. We all got a woman, don't we?"

Benneteri wasn't letting it lie. "Yours?"

Jared thought on the skimpy little bra he'd grabbed when he last left Pauline's bedroom.

She and Tom having it out in the kitchen, and Jared shaking himself into his clothes fast as best he could, wanting to trash the place but refraining from doing so, and there peeking from the half-open bureau drawer, Pauline's lingerie. He took it, he just up and stole the lacy thing – a bra, cream and pink interwoven lace and cup and satin – enough to make a man come just palming it, while conjuring the right thoughts, her sweet deft touch.

"Yeah," Jared said to Benneteri. "I got a girl outside."

"Yours?" Benneteri said again.

Don't know why Jared confessed to this slick gray stranger but he said, "Married."

"Ain't that half the time the problem?"

Jared nodded.

He'd brought that piece of Pauline with him in his front jeans pocket all the way to California, had it on him when they processed him here in Lincoln County. It went with his possessions, with his watch and his skinny wallet and his boots when they bagged them up.

The jail authority looked at him and all she said, while noting his belongings before she locked them in a cage all their own, was, "Hm, hm, hm."

From the cell across the way, one particular scum-drum yelled, "You think I don't see you? I see you, motherfucker!"

Benneteri leaped up.

Shakey, rounding the table, rushed the bars. "You're lucky I'm not over there, I'd beat your fucking ass."

"Yeah, and you have a nice day, too, piss-ant."

Shakey held on and rattled the cage. "I'll fucking kill you. I'll catch up with you, motherfucker. When I get outta here I'm gonna kill you." He kicked off his sandal and threw it at the door.

Esther and her buddy guard, Peters, showed up. "You want solitary?"

Shakey said no.

"Well, then knock it off. Happens again, I'm going to haul you out of there."

Esther and Peters stared down Shakey, observed the cell's six-pack of sad sacks, and then they left.

The guy sputtered while dialing his volume low. "Fucking bitch. Fucking watching us on the TV. Voyeur's what she is."

Shakey amazed Jared with his vocabulary.

His bunkmates were lesser criminals waiting for justice to roll through, just like Jared, without the money to bond out. He listened and learned, eyes shut, ears tuned, never quite easing into the release true rest offered. He wrapped up as best he could, under the sheet and then the skimpy blanket, sleeping in his orange jumpsuit, fending off cold and the pervasive damp, the kind that accrues in a tomb, the kind that builds bad dreams.

Dreams that featured Basement Brent. Future poet, future rapper, future pedophile, future fuck-up, future user. He cut his teeth on Jared, sharpened his fangs, sucked Jared dry. Jared, Brent's private prisoner; Jared, coming and going as he pleased, prisoner of curiosity and hush-hush all in his mind, and yet bound, stuck attempting to be a best boy, though he'd never describe it so.

This came from within, this structure and instruction, his only dad-like kin had ever been Sten – no wonder Jared worshiped him and did whatever his brother said, or whatever he thought his brother would want him to do, would applaud him doing.

Sten had no pro or con about Brent, he hardly knew Brent, though the guy was from the neighborhood, and maybe Sten suspected something, but he simply said to Jared, "What're you hanging out with that fuck-head for?"

Jared wasn't about to toss this single friendship made on his own just because Sten questioned it, or, perversely, he held to Brent more tightly because Sten had a burr up his ass about the two of them palling around, probably ticked about being replaced.

Brent unsnapped the world when he unsnapped his jeans. Jared imagined the dank basement air rushing Brent's exposed parts. This was not right; also uplifting and goose-pimply and forbidden, and no Sten to the rescue. They were utterly alone in a dungeon where Brent had five years and fifty pounds on Jared.

And how many times had his mom railed at him "Do what you're told"? Nothing like this in Sten's experience, Jared would bet, so he tarried with an inkling to hang, to step a footprint where his brother hadn't.

At the same time, he wanted freedom. The duality of the twitchy forked branch seeking water, seeking escape. With his head pushed down to Brent's crotch, Jared grabbed the guy's ass, just to gain balance – hey, he was a puny ten years old! – and Brent pinned those hands behind Jared's back as he lifted his pelvis.

Jared, with his hands cuffed in Brent's teenage-grip, got backed up to the crumbly foundation wall, rock over-painted by dozens of tenants and owners in the last ninety years. Three other times, that's all, and each time, Jared believed, under duress, cornered, captured. Brent elicited new imaginings, seamy and slimy and perpetually of the earth, and like the basement walls, weepy.

This was jail, and this was what jail brought back to Jared. The Vicodin had him tripping, too.

After his oral surgery, still woozy with anesthesia and clocked by the pain meds, he met with a public defender. He'd pled guilty at the arraignment, so there wasn't much the dude could do for him. All life was a fucking formality, except for Pauline.

That's where his grace lay, what Jared had a mind to claw back to, even if right now it was a fuzzed-up desire. His hands scratched the counter top like it itched as he watched everybody's lawyer through the dividing glass.

"Probation's revoked," the guy said.

"For sure." Jared heard his thoughts, but couldn't voice one of them without sounding like a Mush-Mouth. He lifted his hand, the universal *whatever* gesture.

"Your sentence from the assault, the judge re-instated. Add the damage from your little California trip, and he's got you up to five. But the mugging wasn't your fault. You were the victim there, and we garnered you some sympathy on that count. With those stitches up the side of your shaved head and the busted mouth and ear, you present a pretty picture. I got you down to two, your time started yesterday. Model behavior and the judge might, I say *might,* think about seeing you again in six months. All depends."

The psychic energy of the place had been tapping Jared out, and the lawyer drained his last drops. His fucking teeth hurt. He had the yellow-haired Nazi for a bedfellow, their bunks bumped heads. Who knows what that psycho's story was?

Six months was plenty of time to learn it, to learn all their tales by heart. By the end of this, Jared would be no good to her. No menace here, only loss and solitude.

The trustee came by with the commissary-on-wheels, and Jared bought a five-dollar phone card on his jail account. Call Pauline is what drummed through his fibers.

And say what? Hey babe, guess where I'm calling from. Turn his life into a joke.

He'd pocket the card, and ponder, because what he'd say had to be damned near perfect to erase her objections. God, how he hated disappointing her. By not calling, Pauline still centered his dreams. Once he called, he'd be done for. She had Tom, and she and he were both on the outside. She probably thought Jared was still in California or westward, no clue he moldered just down the highway, behind razor wire and bars, with lunatics and deadbeats.

All the things Jared expected about jail, details soaked up from movies and other prison lore: smoking, the bartering with cigarettes for Christ's sake, and outside exercise, shooting hoops in the yard, a weight room – none of that here; no yard, no outside. Maybe twenty mangy paperbacks were available off another cart the trustee rolled through around seven each night, a pitiful selection you put more of your shrinking jail funds to, like the chocolate bars and the chips and the toothpaste and the disposable razors his cellmates plucked from the commissary "truck." Everything had its price.

From the one TV outside in the hallway, Jared could catch sight through the bars of the game shows that played, or NASCAR or *Sports Center* and, for gray-haired Benneteri,

Sponge Bob. Another kook.

"I want to live in a pineapple," Benneteri said.

Nobody dared cough a laugh.

Jared eased his body back onto his bunk and tried quelling the hurt in his head. He planted his gaze on the start to an old book whose cover blared it had been made into a TV miniseries. The yellow-headed guy took the same reclined position on his bunk, bookless though, the tops of their heads so close their hairs could have messed together if Jared's hadn't been shaved when the California docs did their stitching.

Packer – they called him Pac Man – started whispering, "What're you here for?"

Jared set the book on his stomach and talked at the ceiling. "Assault. And then busted probation."

"That's royal," Pac Man said. "I'm a B & E man."

Man? The kid couldn't have been out of high school. "How old are you?"

"Twenty."

Jared said nothing.

Pac Man went on, "Me and my friends did this house. Ritzy."

"Except for Chicago and those north lake suburbs I didn't think this state had ritzy in it."

"No, man. Down in Wheaten there's a section we call Diamond City, estates and shit. All kinds of land. Mercedes coming and going."

Jared let him go on.

"We got some good stuff, primo electronics and shit, you know? Making contacts the next day, to unload it fast, and meanwhile one of the dumb fucks—"

"A buddy," Jared said.

"Yeah, one of them idiots gets busted for lifting liquor

and so he rolled on the rest of us, to try and sweeten his own deal. So me and my other guy – there were three of us – we boosted a car, stuffed all the stole shit in it. Free and clear all the way to Wisconsin, baby."

"But then?" Jared said.

"Well, we were drinking, and Matchick was weaving, or I guess at least driving suspicious enough for the trooper that pulled us over. Man. Been here six weeks, pled guilty – hell, we were caught red-handed. Don't know my sentence yet. Fuck, I'm still waiting for a sentencing *date*. But I ain't in no hurry, you know? Ain't going nowhere."

"Nope."

Going nowhere. Jared could relate. He was ten years older than Pac Man. He shook his head over the kid's stupid jump to stash stolen goods in a stolen car, then drink while hot-footing across state lines. Truth was Jared had been world-wise and weary at too young an age. Pac Man was no Nazi; he was a buzz-cut kid, a screw up, but no deviant.

"What's that up your back?" Jared said.

Pac Man grinned and pulled at his neck with his fingers like he was trying to catch sight of a collar tag on his skin. "You like that? It's a map of the goddamned Bahamas. With ship sails and anchors and birds and shit."

Tame, adventure-boy icons. Tattoos could mislead you, except for the creep Jared pulled the knife on. Serpents coloring the skin of that DairyMart fuck clued to his character. The guy was a goddamned snake.

"What're you readin'?" Pac Man said.

Jared lifted the book, looked at it and saw Pittsburgh sewers, saw California mud, saw Pauline in her boots modeling pearls in the Goodwill Store. "It's named *Rich Man, Poor Man.*" His mom paid Jared to paint their basement when he was fifteen and grousing no one would hire him without a job permit. He wanted to buy a new deck for his skateboard. He wanted money for a Walkman. He needed things.

She told him, "Scrape first. All that peeling is a mess. You might need to sand, too." Three and a half walls, the rest of the space occluded by the washer, the dryer, the stationary tub, and steps to the upstairs. She didn't know what she was talking about and neither did he. This wasn't thought-through renovation, but a chore to quit his pestering. He bought sandpaper, a ludicrous tool he worked the morning with. After lunch, he started shaving with a wallpaper scraper. Bent down and balanced on his haunches, Jared addressed floor level where Brent had written in pencil: Sex is good; sex is power.

Jared spent greater than average time smoothing what he could of that one stone. He ended up wiping down all he'd managed to treat in one day and the next threw thick coats of paint at it, called it done.

A long line of perps had written on the one jail crapper wall that held the toilet paper. A few particular words among the many stood out: God helps those who help themselves. He read it every time he squatted and each time he pissed, and it rang as true to Jared as Brent's claim of power.

All souls on earth were clueless about that basement business. Jared told nobody, and Brent sure never spilled, though surprisingly he didn't brag either. Then again, bragging might have squelched opportunity, which occurred that one summer only before Brent's family moved to West Virginia. Further up the future, Sten met the army, Afghanistan, and maybe his grave, ignorant of all that went down when Jared was a boy looking for approval, but in Jared's head Ghost Sten knew and his voice was not wisecracking.

Though his live brother had cemented a reputation for serious ass-kicking, Ectoplasm Sten oozed sadness.

It hadn't marked him. A man lives through and puts up with a lot of crap, but it doesn't mean it's character forming, at least not detrimentally. Everybody fights against their own darkness. You could choose to do good, be good, be better than what your past projected. You always had a choice.

Jared's mouth felt like a blown-up minefield. He drooled blood when he slept. Fear, which he hadn't much of, even in jail, sparred with him in his dreams until he didn't know which end was up. Dizzy when I met you, he'd tell Pauline. Dizzy still.

He touched the phone card in the pocket of his jumpsuit, and sought warmth on the stale mattress. Around the picnic table, Shakey trudged his 3:00 a.m. groove. Jared was not sure how many days he had been here. It had been a drugged-numb routine from the get-go. Pac Man and The Gill Man, who survived an attempted drowning by rival thugs because he could hold his breath preternaturally long, and gray-haired Benneteri and Hardwick, whose story he had yet to learn, all snored and slept through.

It took no close tuning for Jared to absorb news of the one other guy who was awake, his pill-modulated pal walking off the heebie-jeebies, and the sound of his wheezing or praying or counting.

To the Interior

The trees of Illinois pierced Pauline with their color. Drought was sending everything early to seed, but it rewarded with brilliance. She steered the Bonneville, with Pendleton beside her, leaning in, friendly and dependent. Things were rounding a curve.

"Autumn might as well be the new year," she said.

The dog licked her face. He didn't know anything different to do.

It felt like weeks she'd been without Jared, but it was only days. Her wanting had been shaving her into her present shape, concave at the waist, and then, yes, a definite pulse of belly where she had always been so taut. Tom used to tease he could bounce a dime off her stomach, like a sergeant testing his soldier's spiff-tucked bunk.

Did Jared suppose she would just forget him? That she possibly could? He was her favorite missing person. He was *in* her and would not be rooted out. She tried not to imagine what he'd been doing, where the hell he was, what he wanted and whether she could give it.

She shut down the big steel door on this idea: He is not for me to have. She wanted him to overwhelm her the way he did.

The gravel of her driveway pinging the car's underside and making her fishtail up the steepest part to the house cheered her. She didn't suppose home was where her heart was, but look, it seemed to be.

"I live a cliché," she said. Corny as it sounded, the sight of the house she owned did swell her heart.

Pendleton *pitter-patted* in place, anticipating the door cranking open. Pauline scanned the familiar landscape – Tom's rig, nowhere. She released the dog, set free her own anxieties, inhaled the blistered air of all that sagged spent around her homestead, and relished the still ground. The atmosphere had sucked up the precipitation so all there was wind blasting through her hair and her road-wrinkled clothes. It blended the car's long-haul diesel smell with the organic breakdown of elements. Pauline opened her arms, stretched them high above her head. It was still summer when she left. Summer had burned up.

At the retirement home, Maudie sat in her unit with the other forgetfuls, shriveled and waiting, as dry as the day outside the multi-purpose room windows. But her eyes sparkled like opaline jewels. Her hands grasped atop a lap blanket Pauline had spent last winter crocheting. The woman appeared determined not to pitch forward despite the curvature of her spine. She always sat like this, accepting Pauline's uninterrupted Jared updates, over which she nodded, working her lips to nothing. She had been the first to hear of the affair.

"He has no visible means – to me, anyway – of earning a living, and little else to offer."

Pauline wavered, she sighed. "Only everything I yearn

for."

He was her mouthful of chocolate.

She carried on just to hear herself talk. Maudie never spoke. After a lifetime of berating and finding fault and belittling, Alzheimer's had sewed up her tongue.

"But it's not for Jared, anyway, to do the offering. I mean, why not turn it back to me, ask this question: What do *I* have for *him*?"

Pauline knew she provided anchor for a moody, brotherless man. "He says he loves me past sanity."

She could imagine, had she made it all the way to wherever the hell he'd landed in California, him saying, "Are you sorry you came?" and before she could answer he'd stretch the fraying line between them further. "You should have stayed away."

Tom stood beside his stepmother's wheelchair and said, "You should have stayed away."

"Good to see you, too," Pauline said.

Maudie clicked her tongue against the roof of her mouth in the way she'd *tsked* at Jared a thousand million times. Some recognition still lived in her and managed to find outlet. Pauline was one hundred percent with Maudie on this judgment.

Tom looked over the heads of the oldies, and tightened his grip on the chair handles.

Pauline said, "Since when did you start showing up here visiting the folks?"

"Since you didn't."

"So it was my job? My family?"

"You married into it, me, into them."

"I married in, and as soon as I did then you seemed to skip out."

"Speaking of skipping out, did you find what you were

looking for? Find him?"

Tom would wound her until she no longer allowed it.

"I bet you've had your fill of us for today, hmm, Maudie?" Pauline put her lips to the lady, tasted the powder on her cheek. Some nice nurse had dusted her that morning. Maudie palsied her hand on Pauline's bent-in-half belly.

The few fairy tales stowed in Pauline's memory washed over her, a book of Grimm and all things that go wrong. She'd hoped her fainting had been left on the road. By her arm, Tom steadied her.

He led her to a hard chair, surrounded by a knock-off brand microwave and a mini-fridge and shelves stacked with Corel. The smell of boiled vegetables permeated the place. The over-lit kitchenette drained Tom's face. To him, she bet she appeared just as blanched.

"You look like hell," he said.

"Gee, thanks."

She gave Tom credit for thinking, now that thinking had been forced upon him.

He said, "Can I get you something? A drink of water?"

"I need—"

"Pauline—"

"Do you suppose I could—"

"I stayed while you went. I've been here this whole time. Isn't that what you wanted to hear?"

From the moment Jared set his coat on her shoulders she'd been walking from Tom.

"I've had time to think," Tom said, "about us. You, me."

She looked at him.

"Is it too little too late? Am I out of the game?"

She set her hands on the table to keep it from vibrating. It was fake oak wood, shiny veneer over particle board. He put his hand on hers. She said, "There's a bigger story now."

He nodded. "Okay. Tell me."

He sat there, angling his head to hers, accepting life at her speed. From where and when had change come over him? Jared was the why. She waited for Tom to ask, wanted him to berate her the way Maudie and Hollis used to lay into him as a teenager. As adolescents in his kitchen and his living room and his basement, she witnessed him take it from the folks, just taking it.

"Should we see Hollis as long as we're here?" Tom said.

Her last dream before she left the Moerleins – or the last she recalled – it was her job, to gather the eggs. In the hen house, she held her breath. She never used to be so easily filled by smells and sounds and elements. Not enough air. The world was not clean enough for her to breathe. She reached one hand to the icky inside wall of the clap-trap building, wondering if balance would be like this from here on out.

Hollis was a liver-spotted old man, shakier every day, but unlike Maudie, he got around with aid from a stick he lifted when his talk turned excited. Pauline flinched each time, and Tom neared her edges like Jared would, aware of her nerves. She wanted her husband's chivalry to mesmerize, but it just made her sad.

"Giving the nurses what for? Been behaving?" Tom said.

Hollis set the rubber tip of his cane at the edge of Pauline's denim skirt and raised it several inches while tilting to peek beneath.

She scooted outside his reach, sat in an industrial formed chair.

Hollis said, "Your mother keeps me in line."

Tom said, "I don't see how that's possible."

Hollis gave him the steely eye. "Don't be knocking your mother. We're fine in our way. Don't need your interfering, your pitiful efforts."

All of five seconds for Hollis to start chewing what yielded the most gristle: Tom's imagined shortcomings. Made Pauline want to slap Hollis right across his whiskered cheek.

She'd been containing the impulse since she was twelve, was cataloging all the times Tom shrank from his father's whip-words and clenching her hand against them when Hollis said, "There's gonna be a change."

Tom said, "Huh?" He'd been skimming through Hollis's skinny closet, lips moving like he was counting.

Pauline tiptoed up and whispered at the back of his neck, "Are you worried somebody's stealing?"

Nearest him she'd stood since her return from the road, except for when he caught her mid-faint. She smelled the soap he used to wash both his body and his hair and aroma of the half-dozen cigarettes he'd probably smoked on the drive over to this place. He hated visiting the folks, she knew, and she wondered how many times he'd sucked it up and done it in her absence.

"They ain't so bad," he said as if reading her mind. Or maybe he referred to the staff.

He said to Hollis, "You need winter flannels? We'll pick you up a few shirts." The specter rose without prompt: Goodwill Store. Pauline endured the stammer it brought her blood. "We should go," she said. She put her hand to her brow and faked a headachy look.

Tom said, "You tired, babe?" His hand settled between her shoulder blades and remained.

"I could sleep." She resisted leaning into him.

"All's we do around here is sleep," Hollis said. "And eat and shit and Bingo. It's enough to make a man one fat cat. And the ratio's five to one." He winked in the manner of "old Hollis." Pauline wondered if he was skidding mentally the way of his wife. And then decided, no, not dementia, just humanity.

She counted Neal and Tom and Jared, her three strikes. Like Hollis, she endured her competing desires.

"Do we have anything left at home?" Tom said.

The flat manner in which he treated their insurmountables stunned her. Then she realized.

"Groceries." The room rolled its wave over Pauline – old people, sickness, medicine, love. She steadied herself with Hollis's cane; she had both handle and his hand.

Her father-in-law gazed through her like he'd slipped into a Maudie-fugue, past her and on to Tom.

"I'll stop and pick up some basics," she said.

"Don't forget the bread and butter," Hollis said. "And milk. A child'll squawk day and night for milk. You did," he said, looking at Tom direct.

Because they'd arrived at the retirement home separately, they took off in their own vehicles. Even with the supermarket delay, Pauline made it home first. Pendleton tailed her inside and outside, the three trips to and from the car. The screen door almost slapped closed on him once, but he learned and scooted fast when he had to.

"Don't let anybody tell you you're not smart," she said to her dog. She ruffled his muzzle, kissed him.

There were things to stow in the pantry, and then in the refrigerator. On the near-bare shelf, a complete six-pack of her favorite bottled beer, sat cooling where nothing else had been replenished. Tom had done this for her. She removed one and let it freeze her palms while she talked to Jared in her head. I will never be the same, she said. And, you carried me above the world. And, Now my feet, they drag the rest of me.

She heard Tom's rig toss up gravel in the drive and she wondered how long she'd been standing, holding the cold bottle. Because she wanted him to think she'd just taken it out, she didn't put it down. Pendleton rushed the door, and Tom nudged inside despite the dog's exuberance. Pen would give you a million chances to love him.

Tom got a beer for himself and then took Pauline's, twisted free both tops, handed hers back.

The last one she'd sipped in this kitchen, she'd shared with Jared after the power failure. Jared: her catastrophe. She gazed at the beer bottle without really seeing it, considered all she would have to give up, then set it on the counter. "I bought a gallon of lemonade." She retrieved the jug from the fridge and poured a half glass.

Tom finished his tilt, swallowed, and eyed her accordingly. "So Dad's suspecting is right, then?"

She pursed her lips. "Maybe sixth sense breeds in that old folks' home of theirs."

Tom said, "Add all that multiplied experience."

"I didn't undergo any official test. Just operating on my gut and my symptoms."

"You're sick?"

"And tired."

"Ha. Sick and tired. Yup, that would be you all right."

"Tom, I can't argue now."

"So we'll argue later?"

He smiled and she couldn't help it, she did too. She just as quickly lost her happiness.

"I thought I knew who I was," Pauline said.

"I thought I knew you, too."

"I'm late," she said.

"I figured."

"They say sometimes stress will make you skip."

He looked at her like she'd made a bad joke.

"What?" she challenged. "Don't deny the amount of stress around here."

Tom retreated, set his back against the opposite wall, braced his weight with his knees. If he wanted to be any farther from her, he'd have to leave the room. To Pauline, he looked collapsible. He drank from his beer while he eyed the floor. Then he lifted his face to ask, "Is it mine?"

"I can't quite say."

"Because you don't know."

"That's correct."

He stood straight to start walking toward her. "Jesus, Pauline. You're always giving yourself away."

"Oh, shut up." She shrank from him. "You think this sits quiet with me? It doesn't. It boils inside whenever I think on it, which is every minute. You don't think I regret?"

He kept moving in until he had her against the sink.

She said, "I'm sorry I don't know. But I'm not sorry I'm pregnant."

"You planned it?"

"Of course not, but—" She couldn't quit when the tears came. She put her hand on his chest where his heart had pumped out a gazillion beats, where it was double-timing right now. She felt the heat of him working at holding back from her. In better days, he used to joke and termed it "the effort of resisting Pauline." She was going to push him away but she didn't need to because he set her free from where he'd blocked her.

"What you've done, Pauline, is unforgivable."

"I'm not asking you to forgive me."

He whirled around to her. "Well, maybe you should! You should at least ask for that."

"Life and love are unpredictable," she said. He would not make her apologize for loving Jared.

Tom said, "Life is twisted and hairy and mean."

So he was calling her mean. She shrugged. It was true.

He put his bottle in the sink. He said, "Come outside with me."

"What for?" She didn't think he would ever hurt her, but she was curious.

"For a minute, just come with me, okay?"

A moon turned the driveway white. They didn't need other illumination. Their boots crunched rocks and litter from the trees and pine cones. It smelled so vast and rich; this was her home. In this safest of places, Tom had learned she loved Jared and now he was acknowledging the baby.

"I know you'd given up all idea of us having a family," Tom said.

Part of one of her songs ran through her head: Walk with me through gravel/stand with me on stones/feet might hurt, for what it's worth/ain't it good to feel grit?/humble down, tumble down/travel me, make me weak/gut me, heal me/ raise me up.

Herron had said, "The thing is, there's never a right answer. There's just the solution that works for right now."

And Johanna, in her goodbye, had gripped Pauline by the shoulders, bored her through with her prairie-diluted blue eyes, and said, "You will persevere, because you're meant to."

"Who says so?" Pauline had said. Who, she wondered,

had the foolishness to promise like that? In returning to Euphoria, Pauline at least accepted what was hers to own and pursue.

"Aren't you going to say anything?" Tom said.

Pauline examined the stars and the holes those stars were burning. She said, "No matter who's the father, I'm the mother. I am going to have a baby – yes, you're right – after I'd given up on that long-time wanting."

There were things Tom knew from having been around longer, and first, that Jared had yet to acquire. It was chilly and she shivered and Tom, being Tom, brought her to him. He nodded as she spoke into his shirt, "I am going to be some poor thing's mother."

The Hard Soft Landing

On her fizzled-out journey to Jared, Pauline had accepted oblivion about any day of the week where she stood. Topography out the window jangled against what she knew, where she'd grown; nothing lined up as it should have. The Moerleins' yard did not grow her grass. The trees bent to different winds, not to mention emotions and a rebel body. You thought you knew your world and the elements evolving day to night and time in between, but you did not know. The planet – that great grinding machine – honed its axis. It had a mind of its own and shoved it on you.

Tom said, "The guy's a con-man, Pauline, and a liar." Being Tom, he had to say that. No string of logic attached to how she felt, only desire to let Jared wash over her the feeling he brought, the feeling of *I am found*.

Herron had advised, "What you've acted on will bring you the comfort you seek."

She could just imagine sharing the reverend's wisdom with Tom, and Tom sputtering, "The hell you say."

The night brought a lull. They'd slept in the same one bed, each hugging their edges, but morning forced them to see what they did not like in the face they woke next to. Pauline pulled a sweatshirt over her pajamas and got up to make coffee, to flee judgments she just bet stacked in Tom's throat. Pretty soon he'd say he couldn't even swallow because of her.

She looked around at the disheveled state of her home, starting with the sink and the overflowing trash can, and said, "This place needs cleaning top to bottom." She pulled on rubber gloves and shook powdered scrub across the basin.

The wood from the cut tree still waited to be moved to a sheltered spot. Her plants up the hill had probably grown to man-size in the enriched soil, while the African violets and the Swedish ivy and the philodendron inside had expired. As the coffee gurgled, she picked haphazardly at curled leaves and then lifted the dead things, pots and all, into the trash.

Pendleton scampered to hide from the crashing clay and her scary, yellow-clad hands. She heard Tom yelling at the dog to "get out from under me."

You have my heart, she'd tell Jared, but Tom captured her promise and he had been first. She was trying to rein herself in. Jared consumed her like an accident she couldn't turn her face from, was whom she'd kept closest, the one she'd made room for. He was the habit she had to break.

Jared said things happened for a reason.

"This isn't one of your goddamned songs," Tom said loudly from the bedroom. "Pauline, this is real life. Happy ending doesn't rain down on you after three or four minutes of a catchy tune with a final, put-it-all-straight verse."

She said, "I can't change the past, and it's useless

wishing. We all know what I did. You can beat me about the head with it at half a dozen different angles, but when are we going to talk about you and your stepping out?"

Tom rushed her against the kitchen sink, tugging his jeans up over his hips, still shirtless.

"When have I ever done anything as bad as you playing house with that guy here? And then you taking off after him?"

"No evidence doesn't mean no crime."

"You can't be serious."

"Why can't I?"

Pauline almost put her hand to his bare chest. She imagined his heart beating there, outside his skin, while her pulse thudded in her ears. She wanted to measure somehow for herself the amount of his caring. He did not set it out often for display, and she'd accepted his subterfuge.

He threw his arms up like surrender, and she flinched. "Who, in this day and age, has unprotected sex?"

"I guess I do."

"Evidently."

"You know how we tried. Why would I think pregnancy even possible when you made me feel it was my fault we were failing at what other people seem to do so easily?"

"Me?" he sputtered. His arms had come down but she thought he might raise one again. The way he trapped her there against the sink, she'd be only able to duck. Dust from the cleanser was choking her. She coughed, and he backed up so his thighs were not crushing hers but definitely keeping her in place.

"We are married," Tom said. "Now you're having a baby. This all stacks up differently than it did last week or last month."

"How? Tell me how." If he would just talk to her in a welcoming way. But she didn't want to have to beg for kindness.

"It's freezing out here. I need a shirt." He headed back to the bedroom.

She coughed and cleared her throat, then raised her voice. "I said tell me how it's different."

Pendleton watched her from where he'd put his face to his paws on the rug, and she watched the hallway for Tom, who did not reappear. She heard a drawer sliding on its runner and his shoes on the floor.

He called out from around the corner and down the hall, "I'm trying to do the right thing."

She couldn't help being snide. "Since you've always been so dedicated to that." They were yelling through the house, from different rooms. It was easier not showing their faces. Pauline at least knew what to expect from this kind of hide-out communicating.

She spoke quietly to herself, or to the dog. "When's the time I get to live what I feel?"

Tom must have been listening. He said, "Isn't that juvenile thinking, Pauline? Aren't we someday supposed to be grownups?" He ghosted the bedroom doorway. He filled the frame. "Hey," he said, "I can change. You can change, too."

She felt the potential shift for them toward a new configuration. Maybe too many beats she stood, staring, while he expected her to melt because he'd given over the olive branch.

He flung himself out of the frame. "I can hardly stand

to be in the same place with you right now."

She started gathering the kitchen garbage into one plastic bag. Tom ducked out the front when she teetered on the back step with it. The door slammed and his rig ignited and rumbled down the driveway, left her unable to say if she was glad or sad over his argument.

In girlhood, Pauline's mother deemed her Cleaning Day's official duster – herself the epitome of clean, Queen Tidy, Miss Spic n' Span. Make it Missus. Married she was, or perpetuated the illusion, anyway, by the gold band she wore. But like Jared, Pauline never knew a father. Like Jared, she'd been too much adored and altogether too much neglected, depending on the circumstance and the whims of one parent.

She toured her house with a dust cloth and wiped surfaces free of grime. Without a plan, she cleaned a table, then a dresser top, the TV, a chair's bottom rung. Each piece seemed to need her more; her furniture competed for her attention and she wept as she met them where they lived. She set about convincing herself that without Jared everything was easier, less encumbered. She already knew it was lonelier. She'd met lonely on the road and brought it back home; she coddled lonely. Lonely would be her baby until her baby came. Dizziness took hold and she rested on the couch and once the whirl stopped, she rose, sick to death of swimming in her own shit.

You try to make work what you've got – Johanna had said this was what made a marriage long-lived. The woman was all about intent. Jared dismissed folks who pointed out you had to "work at" a relationship. "There shouldn't have to be work involved. What's between two, if it's genuine, happens. It happens and it happens again, and happens constantly, it can't *not* happen. Work's got no part in it."

She had to change the sheets, which still bore his scent from the one time they'd slept here together, which further convinced her Tom had not been home while she was away. Her pajamas touched easy at her waist, but Pauline would soon enough need some different sizes. The notion of Goodwill shopping distracted her from touching each panel of sheet fabric and wanting to stuff it in her mouth.

The Goodwill idea wooed her like an open sore. It got her out of the house and away from the washing machine chug-scrubbing the bedding. And after choosing this and that second-hand thing among the brightly lit aisles, the sparkly cast-offs at the jewelry counter wooed her, too.

The girl who'd once shown Pauline pearls said, "Did you hear about what happened to that guy? You know, the one who bought those?" The sales girl pointed at Pauline's neckwear. In her voice Pauline could hear the thrill of gossip churning the girl's words so, she could barely speak the news fast enough.

In this way, she learned Jared had been returned to Euphoria. Even in shackles, she craved him. In shackles, she maybe craved him most of all. She drove directly to the jail, not sure they'd let her in, didn't know the visiting protocol. Was it like the hospital, with restricted hours and age limits and only next of kin? She wasn't, in any way, his family. In her head, no word for explaining who she was to him.

Jail sat at the rim of the abyss, and at the rim of jail sat Jared. Pauline imagined the place lonely or too populated, either way surroundings that would, over time, bash in a man's spirit. She shivered on his behalf, as well as from the exaltation and fear coursing through her while she walked the gray halls behind the *click-clack* of an authority, about to turn a corner, and into him, as close as incarceration would allow.

Jared watched her enter the visiting area, closing the long-held gap between them, crossing the space, polished, pressed, looking damned fine. She wore a skirt that swished its hem on her lovely knees when she walked and an untucked blouse. He never knew her to wear skirts. Her boots had been swapped for low-heeled ballerina shoes. Her lips were crimson. She was a femme fatale from an old Robert Mitchum movie, set to contract him to do some dirty work: tailing her husband, snapping pictures for blackmail and her later leaving. Tom didn't know it, but he was headed for the divorce bench. Jared could speculate the impossible. He had all the time in the world to deceive himself.

Pauline noted him watching as she stepped in and so she accentuated what he had to observe. He looked, in comparison, stripped and unguarded, almost like a mangy dog. She bit her tongue. In her she had such a capacity for wounding, and her uncensored thoughts would especially dig into him now. If she let out her anger with him, he couldn't stop it and neither could she.

For a while she'd known bliss. For a while she'd been totally adored. But that was Jared's to give and his to take with him when he went. If she considered herself starved, now he appeared the underfed one, too youthful, gangly – an abandonment of his physical self that set her off.

"What happened to you?"

She wasn't giving him a chance to resist the avalanche he'd buried her in. She was going to make him wear it awhile, wear the bruises on his boniness like a hanger wears a suit.

He was determined to work this without emotion because fever wouldn't get them anywhere but crazy. And he didn't need Pauline mad. These few minutes with her he wanted to be sweet so he could re-taste them later in that cesspool of a cell. He said, "No need for that cutting tone."

She said, "What do you expect?"

"Just you, honey."

She looked away from him and at the room's farthest corner.

He stood and smacked both his whole open palms on the divider to draw back her attention. The stoic guard re-crossed his arms; he was ready to move in at a moment's notice. Pauline wanted her hands to meet Jared's, even with the plastic between, yet she clasped hers more tightly in her lap and said, "Sometimes I think loving you is a lesson I had to learn."

"Like a math proof? Proving lies?" He let his hands slide down the glass, embarrassed in watching them fall.

"No. Lies defined me and Tom. With you, proof verified what I'd always dreamed."

"What are you saying?"

"I don't know. There's a time for staying and a time for walking away?" She mocked a high falutin' attitude, got to her feet and pretended she was going, but knew she was fooling no one as she toured the visiting space, contemplating the walls as if pictures or directions hung there, then returned to the straight-backed chair and peered through the scratched-up divider. "Do I haunt you even half as much as you haunt me?"

His Pauline was all earnestness; she was the woman he knew like he knew night on his skin. "Yes, you haunt me."

"At last, truth."

"You want truth? Let's face it, Pauline. You were never coming down from that porch to join me."

She slapped her hand against the counter and leaned her face so when she spoke the partition fogged over in the shape of her mouth. How he wanted to kiss that mouth.

"No! You have no idea what was in my head and what was going on inside me. You didn't know, you never knew, and you don't know now." She liked to think she'd have come down. She was pretty sure she would have.

He looked at her with the greatest detachment he could muster. He observed her like a zoo specimen, a rare bird. He said, "Why don't you tell me? You can see I'm your captive audience."

She let out a cry. "What have they done to your hair?"

Jared touched his head with a ginger, open-palm pat. "The stitches," he said. "Once they shaved where they sewed me, I said, 'This looks like hell, make it even all over.'"

"You look like a convict," she said. She covered her mouth, whispered, "Sorry."

Her lovely teeth, hidden. Her tender voice, occluded.

He said, "Take away your hand. I've missed your smile."

"I wasn't smiling."

"But you will."

And she did. Seeing him brought her back to Square One. Had she resolved on the drive over here to be decisive and logical? Toppled. Even in an orange jumpsuit and Jesus sandals, and with a wall intervening, she wanted him.

Jared said, "If you tell me to bug off, you won't have to tell me twice."

She stared at him for three long beats, then said, "Doesn't look like you're going anywhere."

They both examined their ceilings, and their rights and lefts, down at their respective shoes.

She shifted the conversation. "Have you got yourself some friends in there?"

Jared leaned back in his jail chair, sighed, and crossed his arms like the guard. "Well, let's see. There's Hardwick, ugly as sin but loves his wife and kids, knows he did wrong by stealing that thou over time from the Wal-Mart where he worked. Swears he's getting out, living clean and doing right by them, for them. Was for them he stole in the first place.

"And then you got Benneteri, who despises his old lady, she who had him hauled in here on domestic violence. She says he kicked her in the back, and he was so drunk he doesn't remember any of it transpiring, hell, he might have kicked her. Says he's gonna kill the bitch once he gets out and then he's gonna off himself. Save everybody else the trouble."

Pauline's eyes grew big as saucers, watching him story-tell; he used to love to amaze her narrating a tale. "There you got it, two sides of the same coin," he said.

"Always a woman," she said.

"Always. You can plan on it." He was invoking the

all-inclusive "you," but yeah, she could take "you" to mean her, too, supposing that's how she saw it.

"I used to be your plan," she said.

Jared's plan may as well have been written on paper like the map of California. Oops, up in flames, there it went.

"I'm tired of talking, Pauline – yours and mine. Don't talk. Do. Just do. Let the doing speak."

She wanted proof; it was as hard for him as for her.

He said, "Calling on you to act a certain way I hoped you would, that was wrong. I want you direct and wholly. But I've discovered I'll do with less. I'll take whatever you can portion me and be happy."

She said, "I thought I could love you and not let it affect me, but you took me apart and I've been breathing with one lung ever since."

While Jared folded his hands she waited. He could have been preparing to plead with her, she hoped he would, but his lips stayed compressed, keeping everything in him.

She said, "I know you thought if things came to light Tom would kick me out—"

"Did he?" No mistaking the hope that transfigured his face.

"No, but – my God, your jaw's turned yellow. Aren't you eating? Or getting sunlight? Is it jaundice?"

His countenance softened. "Honey. They worked on my teeth when I first got here." He touched the business of his slow-growth beard. "Just fading bruises from that." He paused. "Can we talk about something else? About what's important?"

"It's all important."

"Has he made it hard?"

"Tom has barely been part of this. It's been on me, all on me. I went after you, you know."

"What?"

She nodded. "As far as Kansas. I was just guessing. I knew the chance of finding you was near impossible."

His excitement got the better of him, what similar thinking they'd done. This was prime between them, the connection that wouldn't quit. Out of sight but never out of mind, of one mind, tangled. "But you were right. I was in Kansas, too. We were on the same road, moving in the very same direction."

She smiled. "The road to here."

Jared grimaced. "The road to jail. Yeah."

They examined each other, then Pauline watched Jared's smile bleed off.

He said, "You're one beautiful sight to this man."

She nodded. She felt her eyes aging even as she watched him through them. "But tired."

"I'm sorry I made you worry."

"Not only that."

He supposed he knew her every thought before she dreamed it. "All that driving," he said, sounding almost pleased she'd lit out after him.

She wanted to suddenly slap him, down-size his ego. She said, "I'm pregnant."

The news became its own wall, ceiling to floor, unavoidable as law and impossible to ignore. In his angular face, Jared's eyes appeared like black river stones. His intellect was at work.

Neutral, but tremulous, he said, "Mine?"

Pauline tried to chuckle, though laughter was not right then in her. "No, *mine*." She sighed. "Wish I could say who's the dad, but I won't risk an amnio. I've wanted a child too long."

This mother-lust of Pauline's, of which he knew nothing, surprised him. It enlarged her in his view, made her capable of greater love, and he'd already thought her the world's most full-hearted woman.

Then Jared shut down a bit, withdrew from her, appeared taller and more gaunt and grave.

"So I was just a means to it?"

"Gosh, no," she said. "It was never a thought in me when I was with you. But if it's the case, then it's the case. If it's Tom's, it's Tom's. Either way, I'm having this baby."

Jared had the sense to know where he sat and was stuck, how he was fucked. Two years serving a sentence from wielding that damned knife on behalf of a girl he didn't know and didn't care spit for.

He swallowed to squeeze down what was climbing his throat. "Tom'll take care of you."

She looked at him, incredulous. "You're tossing me out, sending me back to my marriage then?"

His sight of her narrowed, anticipating and ready to hold hurt a few inches outside himself, depending on what she said next. "Is that what you want?"

"Of course not. Do you?"

His head was an expanding balloon. "I want you, babe. You're all I've ever wanted. I've never wanted a woman like I want you, Pauline."

Which placed them good as nowhere and all the way lost.

The guard uncrossed his arms, tapped his wristwatch, cleared his throat and called, "Time."

Jared felt the chill of his cell a-creeping, but he held a plain expression, while his mind judged that if he couldn't even be honest with Pauline about his fear in leaving her then what was the use?

Pauline had one of her bouts of dizziness so she stayed seated, even with the guard approaching Jared. She said, "Will they let me come here again?"

"I don't know why not."

"Will you see me if I do?"

He smiled. "Honey, I got nowhere else to go."

If only he would *ask* her to return, tell her he needed her, give her something real of himself she could take out of this place to nurse at home and bring back in one piece to show him, so he'd know how vigilant and full of care she was. It had been the oddest visit, wobbly like a table that just wouldn't sit right. Something wrong with a leg. Something off.

When they took him through the door she could hear the noise he was returning to; it raked her skin. She thought of wax that sculptors practiced on before shaping the more expensive raw materials they'd make into art. Jared had taken a gouging. Forces that pushed against him – being shut away, prime – refashioned him. He was changing; he had already changed.

Pauline was snapping the clean linens in the air when Tom returned. She first heard his rig churning gravel, then the doors opening and closing, puncturing the silence. He found her and took up on the other side of their bed, motioned "gimme" with his hands, and began helping her wrap the mattress in the fitted sheet and then tucking in the flat one.

"This isn't chivalry, I want you to know," he said. "It's only fair we help each other when we can. And make this right."

"Are you talking about the bed?"

"I'm talking about all of it. Us. We. Me and you and the family we're having." She examined him for teasing or a lie, for the lapel button that would squirt water so he could say, "Gotcha!"

"You're done, right, Pauline? You're not going to see him again, are you?"

There had been a partition so there was nothing of Jared on her for Tom to smell. But seeing Jared made her molecules spin, seeing him rearranged her. Tom could maybe sense her spinning.

Lies wouldn't help. "I just saw him."

"What? Where? He's here?" Tom scrutinized her. He had a little defeat in his voice.

"It's why you're so dressed up, right?"

She sat on her edge of the bed. "He's in Lincoln County."

Tom leaned on his side so the middle caved, bringing her a little closer. He laughed.

"Really? No, really? He's a criminal? Pauline, you never told me he was a criminal." His tone half contempt, half glee. Boozy breath, glassy eyes.

"You need a nap," she said, standing. She imagined this as practice for handling a child.

He reclined on the freshly made bed. "Yeah, I think I will. You want to join me?" He stretched out his hand but Pauline let it exist there until the dead weight it became made it plop to his side. He closed his eyes. "What the fuck ever."

Tom thought he knew what was best for her. Neal and Jared, too. All these damned men, blinded by their macho crap mixed with the diesel of their hormones, they cited what was best for Pauline, turning her head, turning her this and that way, shoving her over to a new square like a piece on a chess board. None of them knew how Pauline succeeded, what she needed to live, how she required touch over talk and love more than commitment. If that made her shallow, then call her shallow. She'd been called worse.

Mano a Mano

If Jared stayed locked on what he'd do once he got free, that might boost at least his headspace from the surrounding jail rot. Maybe he could petition to work some detail while behind bars because this damned sitting around doing nothing all day was going to kill him. If he didn't kill someone first.

The guys, the men, his cellmates, his buds, the shitheads. They irked him, they set him off, they razzed him, he felt sorry for them, they milked his guilt and his doubt, his sympathy, and his good graces; they fucking pissed him off. He believed their stories and he called them all damnable liars. The place was a crazy house, so why not act crazy?

He eyed them each when they took their turns at the phone, hungry as he was for a taste of outside. Nothing else but the TV to insist anything churned beyond this basement, that the world kept turning.

Phone was a lifeline. They'd been wall-installed in each cell, eliminating the need for guard escort, which they did otherwise goddamned everywhere. The phone card bought from the nightly commissary could connect you; phones probably paid for themselves and then some. No calls came in. Pac Man talked with his mother every night, like a last tuck-in before lights out. Early lights out, they were – nine o'clock, which stretched each long night even longer.

No furniture, so talking with your loved one, you had to stand or sit on the floor. Shakey took his turn and you'd bet the fixture was going to trigger right out of the wall. Sounded like he talked to a brother or a cousin. Hardwick cooed every weekday at his wife and his kids once they got home from school. Gill Man had a sweetheart he called, girl looking to ride his gravy train, he said. Benneteri's wife wouldn't pick up.

Jared called no one. Pauline's single visit had sucker-punched him so he didn't know what to say about her or himself or the baby. Every day he hoped the guard would stroll by, hit the door with his stick and call, "Sarowski, visitor." He anticipated the heads up, and the chance to see her, like that first hit of a good smoke, all his cells desirous, and he guessed Tom, if he had any influence, worked equally against it.

This place bred sleep. Might have been medications keeping the inmates half calm, but also boredom. So fucking boring. Jared employed the time to think on his future. Before prison, before Pauline, even before the knife trick, he'd been a decent heating/AC tech. He could do that again, wanted to be productive, to estimate a situation and solve easy problems of comfort in strangers' living rooms. And get paid for it. Maybe get paid most of all, since it didn't escape his scheming that Pauline and the baby were going to need support. Sure, she had the house and her song residuals, but it wasn't going to be enough. If he challenged Tom, he'd need to bring stability to the picture he proposed.

Proposal. The word turned him on, which helped dent the jail chill. He lay back on memories of Pauline until she was every thing and all things, swooned over her night and day, took to the shower so often the guys banged on the sides of the flimsy structure like it was a goddamned drum while he wanked off. There could be worse ways to release aggression.

A unit's compressor was the heart of the system. The untrained might have thought the thermostat ran it, but the compressor made heat happen. The compressor kept the whole thing chugging along, pushed warmth through the vents, turned floor to rafters toasty.

Jared said to Esther, one day when she took away their lunch trash, "I'm a trained tech. I could work on this heating system, and maybe check out why it's permanent chill in here. I'm not conning you, just offering my services."

She dumped what she'd collected in a black garbage drum she wheeled along the hallways between cells. Then she looked up, her big hands in the disposable gloves empty, her meaty fingers ringless, a scar the size of a lipstick but in the shape of lightning at the inside of her wrist where sanitary ended and flesh began.

"No, thanks, sonny." She smiled. "We like it just how it is." A sweater covered her name tag on her work shirt. She was comfortable with the chill.

Gill Man said, "Hey, what? Now you're trying to make it with the guard?"

His cellmates broke themselves up with laughs and hoots, inciting the cells up and down the hall to pour theirs on louder, like a fucking call and response at a church, any reason to open your mouth and hear your own voice, claiming this place, at least this pitiful place, as yours.

Jared wanted to bust something. He went to his bunk, closed his eyes to it.

One day passed mostly quiet, the TV noise numbed by a swami mind trick Jared conjured so he could concentrate on the *Rich Man, Poor Man* he was plodding through.

"What the fuck's so interesting?" Hardwick said. He popped the battered paperback right up out of Jared's hands. They looked at it splayed open on the floor. Then the prick, a buzz head like Pac Man, served up a loony grin; Stephen King type of loony, that showed teeth better left hid.

Count to ten? How about a fucking hundred, and then a hundred more? Coping that Sten had taught him, he used it now. "Imagine an Elysian field," Sten had said. Jared, twelve and happy with cussing like a street punk, had said, "Fuck the Elysians. Ain't they all dead now?" He'd thought they were an ancient tribe like Spartans or Phoenicians. He didn't know then Elysian meant paradise.

Jared, still reclined in his bunk, said, "You want to pick that up?"

Hardwick contemplated the ceiling stain before eye-leveling Jared with his gaze. "Don't think so, nope."

Jared nodded. He closed his lids, then he leaped from the bed and snap-stood toe to toe with the prick before he could saunter off superior. "Don't fuck with me, man, and I won't fuck with you."

"*You're* warning *me*? Oh, that's rich."

"Ain't none of us rich here. None richer than the next. We're all poor sons of bitches. And we want to keep what little we got. You got some dignity left? Keep it. And I'll keep mine."

Jared bent for the book, and more than half expected the guy to shove him over onto his knees, kick him in the ass or even grab between his legs. Some would say he seemed to be offering it, and he didn't care what it looked like if the posturing gave this cracker a way to back down without losing face among his cronies so the two of them didn't stomp and cut each other and end up in the cooler. He straightened, clutched the book, and up close breathed into Hardwick's face. "Don't make me beat you down, man."

Hardwick two-stepped, then got jolly, turned around and said, all guts and glory to the cell crowd, "He's fuckin' apologizing. Okay, I accept your apology, motherfucker. And quit strutting your ass in front of me like some damned preening bird."

Jared already retreated in his mind, Jared already, for now, checked out. Jared gone back to reading his book on his bunk.

And noisy? Jesus Christ, the place was noisy – like a daycare center or a psych ward, always some kook whining, tantrums, the slamming, the threats and the yelling.

Another afternoon, Pac Man leaned close and said, "We can bug outta here for a few hours for the AA meeting. Wanna go?"

Jared said, "Not interested."

"Who is? Like everything else, it's a game."

"Nah, I think I'll stay here." He lifted his read to prove he had a better date.

"It'll be fun, let's try it."

Exactly what Brent had promised in that Pittsburgh basement. Jared found how much fun that was – like a tar pit. Fun you never quite washed clean of.

"Come on, man. Get us outta this shit hole for a spell."

"Rather not."

His buddy's blue eyes flared. Jared thought the kid might want to fight about this stupid clash, wondered what the fuck did matter to Pac Man other than skimming and scamming from those who had more—which, in his case, was just about the entire universe. Went without saying drink had him by the balls, but did he have contrite shimmying up inside him trying to beat out thirst? Maybe he just wanted a pal to Twelve Step it so he didn't have to walk alone. Fallacy; everybody knew the route to sober was solo, you treading the fine line, hour by hour, marking clean days on the calendar, fingering the coin in your pocket, phoning up a sponsor, sitting in the spill-your-guts circle, ring of coffee and cigarettes and sweat.

He'd witnessed his mother's share of highs, cries, and relapses. She drew you into her bewitchedness, made you a helpmate in it whether you'd signed on or not. He'd been to the grocer for her beer, been to Al-Anon with her, for her cure – whatever. She told him, "You're too damned impulsive and nothing good can come of it." That was one of her lucid days. No matter what camaraderie you landed among, and no matter how much time you sat there trying to amend, at night you entered the door alone. You lay down alone, you muffled the urge; you woke up throat-scorched, soul-scorched and alone.

He said to Pac Man, "Let me finish this chapter."

And he went with the kid to the meeting. It felt freeing to face four different walls, even if they did get guard-escorted one by one. Same color cavern, same peeling rot and stink of cellar and men closed in with themselves, but the room had chairs and prayers, and no droning television.

Forget what you're thinking. Jared wasn't headed for

the jackknife turn. He was thankful for quiet and that's about as far as his thanks hit. He found the surroundings bearable. He estimated the group leader pleasant enough, though he wondered what the jail could have been thinking to let a female in here to try and convert this crew. Not homely, but not a knockout either, not like Pauline. With her willowy kind of build, this woman didn't look strong enough to whip any degenerate into shape, but then she spoke and her voice corralled them like palominos that'd been waiting on a certain type of shelter, *any* shelter. She intoned the Serenity Prayer so it sounded sacred. She had a partner, a guy carrying too much weight for his frame and who'd lost most of his hair. But he'd be plenty enough to pound you if you got out of line; him and the guard at the back of the room double-teaming.

She introduced herself as Cathy.

Pac Man whispered, "I think I'm in love."

Might have been days since Jared found anything funny, but he grinned now at Pac Man.

"Nobody gets out alive," he said.

Cathy walked with a book of verses open against her chest, among the half-dozen of them in their seats huddled near the coffee – pot brewed, none of that instant mixed with your cell's hot tap water. AA had the drip coffee draw, never mind the salvation. Cathy talked like a storefront preacher. "Learn to give what you need and you'll get it."

"Jesus Christ," Jared said, and she turned on him with steel in her gray eyes.

"You got it," she said. "Now how about putting some humility in your approach?" This woman funneled power for shaming; he felt it burning his face. It made him want to challenge her simpy platitudes.

"So all the things we say and do mean nothing?"

"I didn't say they mean nothing. I'm guessing they don't mean enough, your promises. Am I right? Even a bit? Because otherwise, you wouldn't be backsliding to the bar the way you all find yourselves doing."

Jared looked at her, brutal and abrupt. "There's more to blame here. Genetics and predisposition. Environment, upbringing. Friends with the means and those who don't care."

"Is that right? Sounds like you're carrying a sackful. Tell me, where does your fault come in? How many more from-the-outside excuses you got? When do you take the heat for your own decisions?"

"Humans are hard-wired to cooperate," he said, remembering a *Discovery* report that must have drained subliminally into his head from that TV outside the cell.

"So why are you finding it so hard contributing here?"

"Lady, I came as company for my friend. I'm no alkie."

She laughed, and her laugh detonated the other five. Laughs all around, passed among the guys like it was bottled beer. "Is that so?" she said to Jared. "Is that just so? I bet you got some other demon then, don't you, twisting you around his pitchfork? Or hers."

Pac Man chipped in his two cents. "I just want to be braver."

To Jared, he sounded like a ninny, or a guy on the make. So much bullshit, either way. But this Cathy, she'd get their numbers, each sorry one of them sitting here, and play them and win the goddamned lottery on account of their confessions. Then she'd skip off wealthy. And who she'd stole from and used, they'd be sitting there with nothing but empty hands, contemplating bleak futures and reparations to society, if and when they got released. He wasn't going to pass her one clue to his center. That was for Pauline and Pauline alone.

"I'm not playing your game," Jared said. He stood, and raised his voice to grab the guard's attention. "I'm ready for my walk back home."

The dude uncrossed his arms as he came toward Jared.

Pac Man said, "Don't be that way, man."

Cathy waved her book – scriptures, Jared bet it was. She said, "Go if you want. Prison's a prison no matter where your body lays."

What a bunch of crap poured down their throats, more numbing than bourbon. Is this what they called remediation, repatriation, some kind of – hey – the Reformation? Jared smiled at his private joke.

"They pay you to make good citizens out of this captive audience? Scrub away the black that's marked us up? A drunk's a drunk, Miss Cathy," he said.

Mean set her mouth; mean Jared bet she didn't let many see. It was she who called out to the guard, in her doggie-roping voice, "This one's done."

"Careful with that proselytizing now, ma'am. I'll get my lawyer in here, civil liberties and all. I know you can't push God on us in a government institution, even if that institution happens to be jail."

"You think you got right on your side?"

"I damn well know I do."

None of the deadbeats here jumped his wagon. Jared, always alone, except for Pauline. Pauline would stand with him through it all, whatever all was. Fuck that dream. She couldn't even get in his car of her own volition. If she had to sneak off from Tom it didn't bode well for them in the long term, did it? But ... Maybe he'd been putting her through too tough a test. Her scent lived in his cells.

Internally, Sten taunted him, "Ever hear of compromise, you shithead?"

This Cathy-chick had no hand in his fate, not even with the stir of her babiest finger. His fate, where he ended up, was, would ever be, Pauline. With her love, she'd rearranged parts of him, and flat-out stole others. She'd walked from the visiting area the one time she'd seen him here, and the simple sight of her back, with her bra straps shadowy inside the loose blouse she wore, released him like vapor, up, up, up.

He'd been wandering as long as sin. He'd wander further if it meant they'd meet at the end. That disastrous morning before Tom's intrusion, when it was nothing like disaster, his Pauline lay beside him with so much sex on her she smelled like a garden. The memory tripped his walk.

He got his balance before the guard caught or crushed him up against the wall with his club, but the guy had that quick spit out, "Don't try no shit with me, punk."

The guard rattled the cage and yelled, "Sarowski, you got a visitor." Jared was slammed by the way his blood swooshed through like it had forgot how to flow. He jumped out of the bunk, but then almost couldn't stand. Pauline, he thought, sweet Pauline. He ran his hands over his head and over the hair that had developed its own fringey style growing in. He knew he looked – well, hell, he looked like a convict – but he didn't care. He took the walk with the guard, watched his sandals slap the concrete, counted how many steps to reach her.

In the visiting area he sat, with the guard at his back, and through the Plexi divider, he watched the door.

Was this Tom, Bad-ass Tom, come to plead with him?

Jared could just figure what reeled in the guy's head, so niggardly about giving even a crumb of information about Pauline and similarly so damned eager to prove Jared was out of the picture, his competition nullified, that life for the married couple moved happily forward, heedless of him and his wreckage. And what greater proof of forward than the pregnancy? Yes, it was developing, damnit, with every new day it was developing and plunging them all forward, no matter how pretty the past, no matter how deep-dug the memories.

"What do you want?" Jared said.

Tom had a wicked smile and he flaunted it, showed all his perfect teeth. "Dispense with the formalities? Okay. Sure. You know what I want."

Jared held off the flinch. "How's she doing?"

Tom stared at him, his mouth working over some great curse he was preparing. "She's sick day and night."

"Well, that's the pregnancy, right? When's she due?"

"She's worrying herself to death over making herself perfect enough, she says, to deserve this baby. To do what's right."

She hadn't said any related such thing when she'd visited Jared that one time. Tom was conning him. Jared's squint summed up his suspicion. He said, "And *right*, what would that be?"

"Come on, man. This is Pauline we're talking about. She takes everything double-triple serious. If you know the least little thing about her, you know that."

"I know how the world affects her."

"Then you know you've got to let her go, man." Tom pushed back his chair and stood.

"Think about it," he said. His grand exit couldn't have

been staged better by Hollywood. Jared sat there, his arms crossed, *not* thinking. Damn Tom if he was going to tell him, on top of everything else, to think. Not even thirty seconds before the guard's gruff shoved at his shoulder.

"I believe your guy is gone."

In his usual bunk-stretched pose, Jared figured the date May, sometime, or maybe April.

The buzzing of his brain practically incapacitated him. Waiting his turn, he listened while Gill Man dripped his candy-charm all over his sweetness on the other end of the telephone line. Jared invoked patience as Shakey lurched as far as the metal cord would let him bounce and back, chugging wobbly words to an unknown. Next he expected Benneteri to pop up, but the guy was either asleep or dead. No harm wishing, right? Jared saw his chest lifting in easy sleep-breath as he lifted the warm receiver and plugged in his card.

Once he got the lawyer on the phone he said, "Tell me again my options upstate, what can move my time to the fast track."

There was a danger in assuming that there was only one outcome to what was currently happening – he thought about Sten's old pissy love refrain: go away to make her come back.

Man, your thinking's twisted, Sten's ghost said. Which was royal, because Sten had been the King of Twisted, his each piece of advice more convoluted than the one he'd offered before.

The public defender, who had no interest one way or the other except for his own record, said, "Do we need to meet?"

"No," Jared said, "just tell me what I need to know, right now."

The guy sighed. Jared heard him shuffling papers and then taking a drink. "The court requires you remain in custody two years. You've served about a month so far."

"Jeez, time flies, don't it?" Jared said, all sarcastic.

The guy cleared his throat. "You might be eligible for a residential program."

"Tell me."

"Well, maybe a halfway house, maybe a boot camp."

"And the difference?"

"In a halfway house, you may be allowed to leave during the day to work at a job—"

"I got a skill. A marketable skill. They, the court, they're big on remediation, right? I could be a productive citizen. I could demonstrate that."

"Okay. If you go that route, if they *let* you go that route, you need to return to the building every evening. Also, there are day-reporting programs, which run in reverse to the halfway house. You attend the program during the day but can return home at night."

"What else?" Jared said.

The guy sighed. He was a reservoir of sighing. He said, "In a boot camp, they house you at a prison facility, and you can't leave, period. You're apart from the general population and in with 'soft-cores', usually first-time offenders under thirty-five. It's run like a boot camp in the military – early morning rising and demanding physical day labor. You can attend educational classes or job-training and you can get counseling if you want it or think you need it."

"Sounds great," Jared said, already thinking how he'd ace this whole deal.

The lawyer said, "Yeah, well, these boot camp programs are notoriously difficult. And failure to complete the program successfully usually ends up where you're immediately incarcerated. You've got to think long and hard about the options is what I'd advise, before you decide anything."

"But I could be out in six months, yeah?"

"Are you in some kind of a hurry?"

"Maybe."

For now, he would turn his back on Pauline. If that baby in her belly was his, he'd turn his back on it, too, to award the kid a better life, a life Jared didn't foul up. And if all this was what he bore and had to bear and would continue bearing for her to be peaceful, he would. He would do it with a hard face and his heart turned to pudding. Being sent upstate didn't matter.

None of it mattered but Pauline thriving.

Our secret, eh, bro? Sten, reassembled from ash, said, The secret, it's ours. We leave her then, in the field with the goddamned doves.

Stay Where You Are

Pauline's house sealed out the damp well enough when the rains began. Rain Euphoria hadn't had, measurable, for almost three years. Rain was all the talk. Newscasters opened morning, noon, and six o'clock and eleven o'clock programs with the breaking weather. Predictions, measurements, updates, exclamations, flooded basements, grateful fields, dancers who could finally put aside their moccasins. Storm drains doing the job county engineers had envisioned. Danger, and the floodplain, which no one had mentioned in seasons. Talk of higher ground. Pauline's house sat on a hilltop. Pauline was fine.

Through the door blew Fiona, rain-streaked, frazzled, and glowing. Was it fair Tom's sister should glow, too?

"Taxi again?" Pauline moved toward the end table for her purse, expecting to have to dash into the rain, grab the cabbie, and pay. Pendleton tensed because the leash sat next to the purse.

Fee shook her head. "Tom dropped me. He'll be up after an errand, he said."

"He's driving you around in his rig?"

"It's what he's got." Fee shrugged and her layered shirts

bunched around her waist.

Pauline plucked at her own top to quit its hug at her middle. Rain drummed the roof. She wondered if it needed patching. The last time she'd gone up the ladder with hammer and tacks; Tom wouldn't allow her climbing now, acting out concern, which alerted her.

Pauline handed Fee a fresh dish towel from the drawer. Fiona rubbed at her short cropped hair. So much product coated the dye job that her drying method made her look like she'd met a light socket, but Pauline kept her mouth shut, and instead bent to peek outside the front window.

"He might have a hard time getting that machine all the way up here." She felt like a widow on her walk, scouting a man's return from sea. It was for Fiona's benefit.

Fiona, who plopped on the couch, watched, and even dared poke Pauline's belly. "Need to go on a diet, sis?"

Pauline recoiled. The baby was prime, the baby was all. Also, she disliked Fee's crack about her figure.

Tom duped them by bursting through the kitchen entrance. "Had to leave it halfway down the hill," he said before anyone could ask. He kicked off his boots inside the door. As he strode through to the bedroom, he pulled his shirt over his head, mopped his face. "Drenched," he yelled. "A monsoon out there."

Pauline heard his belt buckle ping the wood floor. Hating that he half undressed in front of his own sister, she lifted her voice, "Fee's here."

"I know," Tom yelled over the rasp of a drawer. "I brought her."

Out of the hallway and into the front room he stepped, and there were the three of them for the first time since the night at Eli's. Tom had the thick kind of hair that stayed back when he put a comb through it wet. He'd tucked a dry shirt in his jeans, walked barefoot, made one big clap with his hands. "So! What? We need beers? I think we need beers, right?" He started to the fridge.

Pauline saw he was going to make a big deal out of announcing.

But then Fiona jumped up from the couch. "I got some news," she said. "Neal's back."

Tom said, "Old info, Fee. Remember? We saw him, too."

"I mean back with me, him and me."

Tom grinned like he anticipated a showdown among his girls, but then he slipped into niceness that lately jabbed Pauline more than the anger she knew he had ready to blow. He set the two beers on the counter and draped his arm around her shoulder. "Her and me, we 're pregnant."

Pauline corrected him. "I'm pregnant."

Fiona said, "Hell. Really? Shit."

Pauline ducked out of Tom's hug. "Is that happy hell or horrified hell, Fee?"

"Just gob-smacked surprised is all. Wow. Hey, I'm happy for you guys. It's what you want, right?"

Tom said, "Sure it is." He twisted the tops off the beers and handed one to Fiona. He said to Pauline, "You get milk, Mama."

She wanted to slap his grin. Instead, she spoke sweetly to his sister. "And I'm happy for you, Fee, for you and Neal. It's what you want, right?" She sat on the couch and Pendleton ambled over then plopped at her feet.

Fiona perched next to Pauline, smelling of nail polish and leather and rain. "Did you tell the folks?"

Tom nodded. "They know."

"And then they forget," Pauline said. "Maudie, anyway."

"God, Mom," Fee said. She shook her head.

Her earrings dangled. Tiny skulls on tiny black chains. Was Neal into that creepy death worship, too, Pauline wondered? Or at least the demonstration, the outerwear? She really didn't care. Neal's sexy dark no longer lured her.

She had two on her worry beads: the baby and Jared, and Tom attached to them both in a way she'd love to sever. Unless the baby was his. If the baby was his, then she owed him, didn't she? Didn't she owe it to him to stay? This place was hers, she wasn't going. If they parted, Tom would be the one to clear out. And then she'd be left with what, with whom? A man stuck in a cell, who never bothered calling?

She could re-visit Jared, and she grilled herself over why she didn't. The premise haunted her like a bogeyman under the bed. If she didn't investigate, she needn't face the unknown. So she avoided the jail route, resisted reviewing in her head their one guard-observed meeting. She slept nights, and she slept days. She blamed the baby: the baby stuck her to the bed, the baby sucked her energy. Herron would have told her, "That's depression, Pauline; you're depressed." But she didn't call Herron. She blamed the soggy weather.

She lounged listless in bed and fiddled with words she thought might have been part of a new song: Rain falls straight down, so leave/window open, door ajar. Call me wicked, wired/woman who can't stop loving/the sun in your breath/sky at your cheek/moon on the rise of your brow.

Tom found her doodles on the bedside table. He said, "What is this shit?"

She grabbed them out of his hands. "Have you no sense of what's yours and what's mine? Of privacy? Jesus." Blowing up at him was the biggest spurt of anything she'd done in weeks, other than feeding Pendleton, and letting him out in the rain, then back in. Just drying the dog tired her. She crumpled the pages.

Tom said, "I already read it. And I don't need to guess your inspiration."

"You think you know everything, but you don't."

"I know this. At least I know this, Pauline." She waited to find out what.

Tom said, "Against the odds, we're going to be family. After all this we've been through, you're getting what you want. Thing is, babe, I want it, too."

"You think a baby's going to change you?"

"It could."

She looked at him, mute, stupid.

Tom said, "Do you think this is one-sided? It's not."

She mocked him with a laugh. "She might not even be yours."

"Maybe I don't care. Either way, what's real is we will be mother and dad. And that will affect the changes in us we both need." He paused, and then said, "When the time comes, we can let it pass. We don't have to do the test."

Pauline squinted and realized, on top of lethargy she had a headache, too. "That's plain ridiculous," she said.

"Why?"

"What if she has a rare blood type or needs a kidney? We need to know who's her father, for medical if nothing else."

"Her?"

"I'm thinking *her* for now, until or unless we learn otherwise."

"So, if he's the one, we'll always be tied to him? That jerk'll always be in our lives? We'll forever need to know where he is, just in case?"

She said, "Yes, we'll always need to know."

The baby would decide. The baby usurped everything. From this moment forward, direction would rest on the baby. Queen and princess, the baby ruled. Unborn, but already it was easy as pie for Pauline to cease deliberating over this good and that bad, and to hand baby the reins, because the very great possibility existed that Jared's location and Jared's situation and Jared's flesh and blood would ever need knowing. The baby fishtailed from one side of her small ocean to the other. Pauline imagined the baby clapping her hands.

She minced her steps among the scads of worms flushed from the grass. Pen stretched his leash its full length, intending to drag her downhill, and Pauline let him pull, her boots splashing puddles, avoiding squish and squelch when she could.

Her imagination skipped ahead to years from now when a child of hers might be out in similar rainy weather, collecting worms in a coffee can, for bait or for pets. She envisioned Jared beside a boy on a bridge above a stream, and two fishing poles, a tackle box, bobbers atop the water. She didn't know if Jared fished; she knew he hunted, had shot at birds and targets with Sten.

Tom had taken to sleeping on the couch, but he'd told her, "It's up to us to make this work, Pauline." In which she had no interest. She didn't know how to work at love for him.

After she'd left the jail, she'd stopped someone in

uniform and said, "Can they contact the outside?"

He'd said, "Sure. They can phone you up like any other free men. Long as they pay for it."

The guy told her of the cards guys could buy, and the phones in place. Jared might be talking to her any time of the day, if he wanted. But she couldn't call in, and he didn't call out to her.

She imagined him arguing, "You could visit me. Where are you, babe? You tell me that." She'd rushed to the jail without changing her clothes or considering her hair; she'd gone directly once she'd learned he'd come back to Euphoria, was brought back by the law. She'd felt in jail there the tightrope he walked. Had there been no divider, she still would have sensed him hemmed in. He'd held back and she didn't know how to twist that into any sort of happy.

As the rain had subsided to drizzle, a baseball cap was enough to keep her head dry.

Pauline wore a poncho from the army surplus store, and waders she'd never gone wading in. Again, the thought of stream fishing. She'd seen it done on TV nature shows. Anybody could learn how.

Pen sniffed where Tom's rig had gouged up the gravel, heaved it in chunks bleeding mud from the rains. Then the dog yanked her west into the battered back bushes that rimmed the woods. The branches whipped splatter in her face, and Pauline called out, "Pen!" but she let him drag her. He'd been housebound for so long. It felt good to get out. She was dressed for wet.

She blended in.

Pendleton led her a quarter mile through hip-high bushes, then through thin woods.

Leaves hadn't begun to fall but the smell of their dying

was in everything wet she'd touched. She pulled Pen close, bent to him and released the clasp on his collar. "Go on," she said. "Run. You might as well." The dog disappeared. The rain increased. She could hear it hitting the branches over her head, sifting down. She removed her ball cap and lifted her face.

Her marijuana grew near here, and she walked in that direction. In the drought-baked years, the plants had struggled to the degree that she and Tom hauled water by the wheelbarrow to the poor things. Tom's interest in a prime harvest increased when Pauline cut him twenty percent profit. Once they married, it was just another chore they tackled together, like the vegetable gardening and erecting traps for Japanese beetles.

The illegal in it jazzed Tom. He joked he might need to start carrying a gun when they toted water. Pauline told him to get real. No one was interested in their small enterprise. No one was around.

She maintained, lovingly, about a dozen females each growing season since she'd bought the place, not in the backyard, but still on her land, at the dip in a slight ridge where they'd start out in the shade of the day and then soak up afternoon sun. To get there she had to bushwhack some, and then zig and zag through the sparse woods. It appeared pretty damned secluded when the place was all leafed out like this. The rain must have cheered her babies to their roots.

Each year she'd learned by mistake as much as luck, read up on methods for heartier yield. All on her own, she managed to learn. Pauline always managed to come away knowing more.

The last time she'd been back this way, along with water she'd lugged two sacks of eggshells to spread at the base of the stalks. She'd brought Jared, too.

"They're growing into real beauties, despite this drought," she said. She felt the thickness of one plant's stem between her thumb and finger. The dozen stood about three feet tall, twelve blowsy-headed women.

Among them, he said, "You're the beauty. You're all I see."

Call it a sappy romantic line – Tom would say Jared was working her, but why not let him work? For once, really, why not believe good could not only occur, but remain?

She was crushing the bag against her chest so the shells crick-cracked. "They're big enough slugs most likely can't damage them, but we might as well scatter what we've got here."

"Not one of them looks sickly," he said. He touched a fan leaf.

She nodded, pleased, as if he'd complimented her body rather than the willowy plants.

"Coming along good so far. I use an old Indian trick—plant a fish under each one. Just the head. We ate trout for two weeks."

Jared smiled a gorgeous, lazy smile. "My girl's so smart."

He helped her with every bit of dig and spread and water, and then they lay outside the stalks. The earth underneath them was hard and hot and cracked in places except for where Pauline had mulched. It had felt like the universe was spinning out from their feet as their tremors receded, as if they could control their loneliness.

They were slow about pulling their clothes on, but before Jared zipped his jeans he pissed with aim at the nearest tree. She cut him a quick look and he smiled.

"See?" he said. "I know some things."

It stunned her, him knowing pissing around the plot and on nearby trees would ward off deer and other curious nibblers. Tom had done the same thing when they dug in the plants in June. The two were competing in ways they didn't even know.

"Who would want to step where you pissed?" she'd joked. "Such a strong brew."

Now the pregnancy gave her urine a fierce smell, too.

Pauline figured she'd check the plants for purple. Timing harvest could be the trickiest part.

Initially, she thought she'd gotten herself turned around, or that the rain had blurred her attention to where she walked. She was alone, even her dog had run away. And the plot she'd lovingly tended was a blank pegboard, all the plants gone, not cut down, but dug around and lifted straight out of the muck.

"Pen!" she called. "Pendleton! Come! Now!"

Pauline whirled around and strode through the pouring rain in the direction of home, while she cried. She kept calling for her dog and slapping her thigh with the leash and whipping her head this way and that way. Her ball cap barely shielded as the rain soaked through to her hair. Under her poncho, her belly growled. She was hungry and she was nauseous at the thought of putting food to her lips. She called again for Pendleton.

"Where are you?" she yelled. "Come!"

Her feet slipped on the damned walnuts thrown by the trees. She almost went down. She didn't know what she was going to do once she made it home. Yes, she did. She would head to Lincoln County. After she got warm and dry and quit her dizziness she would visit Jared. Maybe he couldn't tell her how to screw Tom after Tom had so screwed her, but he could tell her he loved her and that would erase for a minute the crop and blight and what all had been trashed. She wished Tom had a gun because she'd dig it out, find him, and shoot him with it.

Walking while bent on thoughts like these in the rain, stumbling on auto-pilot, she wrenched an ankle and her knees wobbled because she feared something bad had befallen Pen. Where was he? And was the law trailing her? Maybe cops had slashed out the crop.

She imagined a gun trained on her by some rabid sheriff, and his bark at her, "Don't move! Stay where you are."

Pauline was done running. Roads out weren't closed to her, but she turned away how a mother does, in that self-sacrificing mode. A child needed roots as much as any one plant. This made her feel quite drunk, though she hadn't had a drink since she took west in search of Jared. She felt really tipsy, like she might fall right over. She doubted her own eyesight. She didn't know who, if anyone, had her back.

She came to the place where she'd veered off with Pen into the bushes, as far as Tom's rig had climbed in the sogginess. His monster tires and the weight of the thing had royally messed up the gravel and everything underneath.

She could be alone. She'd done alone before – hell she came to this place alone, bought it alone, managed it alone. Then a time arrived that opened her up, Jared did it, and she thought she could trust, that giving herself away was safe to do, and that her life would change. She patted her belly. Well, it was certainly changing, every day, those cells spinning inside. She refused to consider what slapped her today had resulted from her own actions or that this was pain she was owed, because she'd had plenty of pain before this and she'd have plenty more after. This wasn't some cosmic payback. This was Tom. This was up and down Tom. It wore his kick-your-fine-ass boot print.

How could he suppose she'd let him stay? Johanna would say, "People have worked out worse. And wasn't his betrayal just equalizing yours?"

The rain swept out the wings of her poncho as she swirled, lunatic-like, on her driveway, churning her anger into one useful current because she was going to need every ounce of it for what she did next. But first, where was the damned dog?

She called for Pen. She stomped across the soaked floorboards of the porch and whipped his leash against the railing. The old-woman look of her waterlogged hands freaked her.

"You come home," she yelled.

Inside, with the door locked, she stripped and ran a hot shower.

She didn't consider until she arrived at the jail parking that maybe they wouldn't let her in. Posted visiting hours limited entry to twice a week, two hours in the early evening. In the way a visitor couldn't just walk into a hospital and see a patient, the jail wouldn't allow her to waltz through the anteroom any old time and see Jared.

She sat forty-five minutes in her car with the radio burning the battery, waiting for six o'clock. The place might have been a schoolyard or a church lot, skirting a building that didn't look to house criminals, but it did. Maple trees across the street had begun shedding. The chain link fence needed new silver. They should put the inmates on paint detail, she thought. The sky opened up and shut. She ran the windshield wipers, propped open the door and stepped out over the puddles.

Inside she stood among others waiting.

One woman said, "Reminds you of the principal's office, don't it?"

Pauline smiled. She said, "Caught skipping class again."

"Or writing on the bathroom stall door."

"Or pulling our senior prank."

The woman's voice got touchy. "Wouldn't know about that. Didn't make it past tenth grade."

Made Pauline a fool for graduating high school. She said, "I feel like I'm maybe going to be sent to detention."

"Except they're the delinquents." The woman pointed to the steel door. "And we're here to give 'em reason why not to be delinquent no more." She smiled, then put her hand over her lips to hide where eyeteeth had been.

The rest of the line shuffle Pauline swore she'd keep her own mouth shut, even though her teeth were pretty much perfect.

"Here to see?" the guard prompted each visitor.

Pauline said, "Jared Sarowski."

The facility flunky typed into a computer. "Are you family?"

"Yes." She placed one hand on her belly, which was in itself becoming a form of comfort and self-medication. Her abdomen had always been a little soft, and now the baby was taking advantage, settling in.

"ID?" the guy said.

She handed it, and he examined it, then raised his eyebrow. Pauline said, "This baby's his," and she played up the sway in her back, the way the pregnancy in its last months would encourage her center of gravity to sink hip level.

The computer beeped and the guy checked it out. He said, "He ain't here."

"What do you mean?"

"Says he's been moved to a different location."

"You mean like solitary?"

"I mean a different location."

"Here? In this jail? I visited a month ago. If he's not here, then where is he?"

"That's information I can't release. Only if you're maybe his mother." He grinned, teasing her, "Are you Sarowski's mama?"

Jared's mother. He had one, everybody had one, but he rarely spoke of her, and never with the kind of love most sons showered on their mothers. The only family he talked of had been Sten. He over-talked that subject. Pauline wondered, a bit wildly, how she might contact Mrs.-Jared's-Mother – wasn't Pennsylvania where he'd been a boy? In a coal town or a steel town. Some kind of dead and dying industry that tore you up to work it.

Another woman behind her said, "You staying or leaving, honey?"

Everybody behind was impatient. If Pauline had been standing back with them, she'd be antsy, too. What's wrong with that damned woman, she'd think, viewing herself as the holdup. Tell her to move it. The rest of us have people we need to see. And the night's getting darker.

She stepped aside. The line processed and she felt thrown from a train, the visceral *umph* and backlash, gravity and velocity kicking her ass. The anteroom to the visiting area held the swirl and dice, noise and density of every dark club she'd ever dashed through with Neal.

People and their goddamned murmur. Buzzing worse than Boner tuning up the amped-in Gibson, and hairier than a three-deep ring of belligerents around the bar. Must she traverse this whole room to reach that itty bitty exit light? The room buckled. It boiled with vicious sea creatures that wanted to be dry and hitched on Pauline's legs like ticks to a hound. She was only one woman, one pitiful rescue. She might never make land, the way she wandered and wobbled, crumpled, went under.

Growing up she'd had no dad. Neither had Jared.

"In the land of the absent fathers," Pauline read to her child on her lap – a golden child, a golden lap, a golden book – "the daddies all drove away in their cars. They had work to do and items to make and people to meet. They were the breadwinners, which means they brought home the bread." She pointed out to her child the illustration of a suited man in mid-stride, his tie-end flying to show his hurry on the page, a bakery loaf in a white bag tucked in his armpit, and the hand at the end of that arm grasping a briefcase's handle. Jared would never work in an office, never don a suit nor submit to paperwork, but he'd bring her bread if that one loaf was the last on Earth. He knew what she needed and he amazed her with his gifts. "Your daddy provides," she said to the child, who looked at her with his eyes.

And then from her arms, Tom took the girl. Absolutely no reason why Pauline had to go on living with his grappling hook under her skin, dragging her sheet of cells back and forth. This misery should be over her shoulder, concluded the way an old rodeo shutters come November.

Jailers shoved smelling salts under her nose and blasted

Pauline's dream to ribbons, loss of story and child. In her mind ghosted Jared's look in the little girl's eyes, erased of bitterness and blame and that chip on his shoulder, the wanderlust and confusion he'd been suffering since Sten – since before Sten, for all Pauline knew.

To the guard, she said, "You'll tell me where he's gone." She didn't ask it as question.

She was a woman with child, who wore bloom on her face and beauty in her bones and in all the soft parts of her more than ever. She'd fainted to the nasty floor of the Lincoln County jail, and because the guard maybe feared if he didn't release where he held and supported her she might mow him down like she'd mowed down Sarowski, he said, "Work release, upstate. To speed serve, I'll bet. Should be out by April if he doesn't screw up."

"He couldn't have gotten me a message?" she said.

"Maybe he was planning a surprise. You worth surprising?"

"Quit flirting and help me stand," she said.

"What? What did I say?"

"Nothing I haven't heard too many times." She brushed at the backside of her jeans, the topmost button of which she could no longer fasten.

She would bet the stolen crop, she would bet her house and her car and the worth of all the songs she had yet to write, that the baby had Jared's genes. She would go to him, she would wait for him, she would abide and reside and be whatever he needed wherever he needed it. She would go to him, upstate if she had to, with not one fade at Tom or Neal or the Pauline she'd been previous. To shut down the cycle of absent fathers, she'd set herself vulnerable, big belly up, no fall back if the man didn't open his arms.

"They allow call-ins there where he is?"

"After a time."

"Has that wait period passed?"

"Probably."

She pulled her cell phone from her poncho, blessing Herron for the world of hope he made her carry in her pocket. She loved the glow the phone emitted when open, blue light putting drama on her mouth as she drew it close. She said, "I'll need his number."

Apart from her, the guard sifted files and maybe even sought permissions. Visitors were reviewed, allowed their turns through the steel door, the numbers thinned, but Pauline bored concentration only on the man behind the glass scaring up her crucial information.

Herron had declared, "You are responsible for each other's happiness." Could a reverend give bad advice? She decided, no. Hell, no. Jared had asked her to be present, and presence was what she was bent on bringing. If another turned out to be the father, they'd figure it so things worked equitably. This one decision presided: she was leaving Tom.

Jared, wearing stale State of Illinois work clothes, another day axed from his jail-hood, his weight on his heels and his spine tensed against the wall, held the phone in a sweaty grip and said, "Anybody with eyes, baby, could see you'd already left."

From Pauline's end, he sounded staked to the earth, solid.

"They got me working," he said.

"How much longer?"

"I'll be there in time for her."

"Her?"

"I'm thinking girl until I learn otherwise."

She smiled, and then quit because he couldn't see her smiling. "You chose this to reduce your time?" she said.

"Chose it for you."

Her steady breath suffused him. He wanted to climb right into the telephone to be beside her and her breath. His spine turned to liquid and lifted free of his backbone. His lungs expanded beyond their norm. The air he took in made him higher than any drink or smoke or drug. His whole being was helium-filled and rising.

Sten's advice had borne out: Leave them to bring them around. "Didn't I tell ya? Chicks, man. You got to learn to trust me." The ghost shook his head, justified, a dim salute fading in the hall end of the halfway house. His last ectoplasmic gasp: Sayonara, bro.

"Is somebody there?" Pauline said.

"Only me, babe."

Sten might be gone but his tape looped persistent inside Jared's brain: Address the bird, man. Means facing the dove in the direction you think she's going.

"I'm done flying off," her voice said on the phone.

Pauline had approached *him*; she had called *him*.

Sten's tape tripped over itself with the excitement of teacher to novice: The incoming bird is the easiest shot, man. The secret to taking her is that you don't pull the trigger until your gun's in the sweet spot – about a forty-five-degree angle above you – and you come from behind. Told you before, blank her out with your gun barrel so you can't see her, squeeze the trigger and continue pulling your gun up. Guarantee you'll take her.

Jared gripped the phone and ground his other hand's knuckles into the fake brick. He shoved his forehead into the wall, too. Trade brother for lover and get free of the fucking basement. The receiver drilled his ear's soft bones with Pauline promising presence, Pauline offering him daylight like it was the necessary fruit, tomorrow snagged on her fishing line, her belly announcing how to be full.

He wanted to believe. Christ, like a convert did, he wanted to believe her.

Go ahead and imagine when and how you'll shoot, but don't you dare move a muscle 'til she's in range.

Jared said, "We got some months to go."

She said, "I'm nowhere without you."

"April, then, I'm coming home to my lovey dove, baby."

She laughed. "Two of us, you'll find two babies here."

God, but her laugh was honey. He conjured her hair and its raft of secrets. He stood firm in the hallway, taking the shot. "What about Tom?"

"Gone."

"Because you insisted?"

She paused, and rolled her, "Nooo. He left on his own. But I'm betting he won't come back after he uprooted and stole my crop. Jar, every single plant he took."

"Oh, baby."

"It doesn't matter. None of that matters. We're done. This gave him good cause for clearing out. Pity he had to take with him all our hard work, but I hardly care about that."

Mean motherfucker Tom. How behind-the-back mean the fucker was, Jared intended taking to his grave. Why distress Pauline over the guy's back-stabbing and his slimy overture disguised as do-gooding? He bit his tongue. In the dark hallway, some of the residents were milling around. The group of them grumbled as they loped to the can, one piece of voice he made out to complain, "Thinks he owns the fucking phone."

He clung to the receiver, would take a beating in a minute if he had to, but right now he simply put to her what he wondered most. "Pauline, what is your best reason?"

"Hon," she whined and whispered. Amazing how she combined those, made them part of her allure. "You. You are my one reason."

He would test her no further, and he wouldn't test himself. He was done with the goddamned examining. He was just going to aim and shoot.

"Others are waiting for calls here, babe. I gotta go. But we'll talk again soon."

Her voice, so small it barely came across the line to him, said, "Oh. Okay."

Pauline continued holding the cell phone to her cheek. She liked its warmth. She'd called him from the jail parking lot, and now she got in her car and drove while the wet that had pounded all day soaked and spread out in the dark. Unable to think, nothing staying lit in her mind for more than a second, she was lucky she made it home. Mentally, she flailed in a whirlpool of detail and review and wonder at what had transpired in her talk with Jared, until, coming up her gravel drive, her headlights swept the porch, catching in them the eyes of Pendleton – alert, devoted, mucked-up Pendleton – guardian of the upended dish. All the birds in her chest bashed out of their cages.

Jared evaded the mob marauding the hall, stepped into the

john they'd just vacated, set his face on the cold wall tiles. He felt like a flame there, breathed heavily, sucking the air out of whatever kind of balloon he'd been upon hearing Pauline's voice.

Sten had patted his aching shoulder in the far away field where they stood as boys, hugging their first guns, "No matter what, there's always gonna be those crazy doves that come in low and start climbing up and away, veering off just as you pull the trigger. You'll miss the bird even though you did everything right."

Jared gagged. Just tutoring, and this, by a ghost who knew nothing of love's enormity, nor knew how Pauline held Jared fixed around her. Sten, exploded by God-centered fanatics, would be forever exempt from learning that lesson. Jared almost buckled under what all his brother would never again taste, but then he wiped his mouth, splashed water across his eyes, stared himself down in one of the silver-pocked mirrors. A hell of an ugly place to take a stand, but on behalf of his brother, Jared shouldered the gun into his sweet spot as if he were a fellow infantryman. He was the shooter and he was the ammo in the chamber, too.

Get a bead on where she'll fall, and then be there.

His old teeth grooved well to his new teeth, but between them he gritted, "She's mine." He aimed himself down the barrel at Pauline, watched his eyes watch his eyes, squinted up and steely, and into a world months ahead of the squalid mirror in this rehab shack, he squeezed off his final fucking shot.

Acknowledgements

Sincere appreciation to my RUCA friends Louis, Sherry and Karl, who read some of IN EUPHORIA in its early draft. Unlimited thanks to David, whose voice rang in my head during the writing, and who is the impetus and the heart.

About the Author

Donna grew up with her sisters on the rural outskirts of Cincinnati. She has been writing poems and stories since elementary school, and upon request she can still recite her poem "Snowflakes," composed circa 1967. Today, she is Development Director of Covington Ladies Home, the only free-standing personal care home exclusively for older women in Northern Kentucky.

Her first two books s with Rebel ePublisher, *At Bobby Trivette's Grave* and *Salt Of Patriots,* have received 5-star reviews at Amazon, Good Reads, and other literary forums. Her work has appeared in dozens of print and online journals, including *Kentucky Review, Watershed Review, Gargoyle, Hinchas de Poesia, Contrary, Southern Women's Review, Change Seven, Forge Literary Review,* and in several anthologies.

She lives in an historic town house in Covington, KY, with her beloved cat and her even more beloved partner. Her two sons and two grandsons live in cities far-flung, and she doesn't see them nearly enough.

Also by this author …

At Bobby Trivette's Grave, Salt of Patriots

And for more from this author …

Please turn the page for a preview of *At Bobby Trivette's Grave*

At Bobby Trivette's Grave

One

High school hijinks, all this back and forth, the ringing and slamming down of the phone, Bobby Trivette's souped-up Charger laying rubber in the drive and then the boy disappearing, angry, taking part of the lawn out with his tires when DruAnn wouldn't skip to his yell of, "DruAnn, come on out here. You know I need you." And when she didn't appear, his bellow drubbed down to decent conversation level, "I need you just a minute." He sounded a little pathetic.

Reece watched from the floor above, with the gauzy drape on his and Bev's front bedroom window held loosely between his fingers so as not to crimp it with sweat.

"What is it?" Bev whispered, probably still half-dreaming.

"The kids are fighting."

"Well, your spying won't change that." Bev rolled

over, opposite to the window, away from him. Nothing new there.

Reece was no voyeur lurking and getting kicks from his daughter's rotten luck, he just couldn't sleep. And interested in seeing how the scene he peeked at played out. Might as well watch, he wouldn't be heavy-lidded anytime soon. Bobby Trivette's antics made the calm invitation to sleep now near impossible.

Reece saw moonlight on the car's front grille show off its crazy metal grin as the boy backed out, sped down the street, ignored the STOP sign, gave it gas, geared up, left DruAnn after she'd run inside, after he'd pummelled the door and she refused to answer. He recognized Bobby's Charger as both classic and familiar.

Even if DruAnn gave Bobby Trivette the minute he begged for, a minute would never be enough. Trying to bully her, he was, and Reece knew his daughter would not bend like a flower to Bobby's sun. The girl had her mother's stubborn streak. This Reece confirmed to himself over his mud-black Folger's and the morning paper. He preferred his coffee strong anyway, but especially so following the 2:00 a.m. drama played out in the driveway, and then the hour or so after of DruAnn's whimpering to herself and sniffling in the room next door, during which no Finch slept.

Beverly had gotten out of the habit of cooking breakfast. She said black coffee sustained her until lunchtime. What he and Bev saw eye to eye on had been shrinking from the start, but they still shared a taste for morning coffee, thick and chicoried. Reece's stomach grumbled as it worked on a meager piece of wheat toast and the hard-boiled egg he'd doused with salt before DruAnn came downstairs. He remembered plenty of big family breakfasts that Beverly served up when Dru was little. Scrambled eggs and bacon, French toast or pancakes. But now DruAnn, in typical teenage fashion, was on a perpetual diet of dry lettuce and cottage cheese and little else.

Reece had no doubt that when DruAnn went out with Bobby Trivette, she succumbed to the drive-in's French fries and maybe even a chocolate malt. How she loved malts. Their trips to the ice cream parlor had been routine, gave this daddy one more way of doting on his daughter.

Because Reece had towered over her, she'd lift her chin, already so opinionated and smart too, somehow aware that eye contact made all the difference, and she'd dig him deep with her surprisingly strong voice. The timbre of it, even at age seven, eight, or ten, hinted at the throaty waver that would later dress up her vocals, and work the bewitching spell that enthralled Bobby Trivette.

Her pipsqueak voice pleaded over and over for a malted during what were then the endless summers of Dru's childhood. Her "Pretty pretty please, Daddy, with sugar on top?" until he gave in. It didn't take much: Reece toppled to DruAnn just as DruAnn collapsed before French fries. And now she had Bobby toppling, too.

Reece watched her sit at the table as she stirred frozen berries into a plain yogurt. His and Bev's eyes met over their girl's sleep-mussed hair, Bev boring into him with her usual stare that telegraphed, "Don't say anything that'll set Dru off." Such nose-in-the air superiority rankled Reece because he didn't need to be told how to step lightly around his daughter. Bev acted like she was the only one able to tune into Dru.

Well, then Reece would break open the subject they

were all avoiding, if for no other reason than to spite Bev.

"Strong boy acting all girl-like." He sucked the taste of coffee through his teeth. He shook his head. "Boy curling up like a worm in the driveway, making a public spectacle for all to see. It's not right, hon."

DruAnn's face flushed the pre-crying pink Reece knew well. A fair girl, her emotions boiled close to the surface. If Bobby entertained thoughts about tying the knot with her some future day, the boy'd have a good indicator of DruAnn's state of mind, and his odds of reception or rejection, just by noting her coloring. He made a mental note to clue the boy in because Reece expected this would soon blow over, whatever spat had bubbled up between those two, and Bobby'd be on the premises again by the next weekend.

"You're not blaming me, are you, Daddy? Because nobody's making Bobby act any sort of way. He chooses the fool he wants to be."

Her lashes darkened with the tears Reece predicted.

"Don't upset her," Beverly told him.

"Me?" In his house, Reece was outnumbered and Bobby Trivette was hardly worth fighting over.

Not the first breakup they'd weathered in these last ten months. DruAnn's temper seemed to guarantee at least a monthly conflict, the girl hard to please and Bobby just doing his dumb-hearted best to satisfy her. Which was good enough half the time. The kids had been dating since December, and Reece kept fortifying his heart to accept Bobby long-term. He didn't care for the boy muscling in on their daddy-daughter duo, but if it had to happen there were far worse out there than Bobby Trivette.

Besides, without Bobby, DruAnn would be moping, or running with Sarah and Jeanine in one of those girls' cars, cruising and smoking cigarettes, Reece knew; though when she did, DruAnn chewed spearmint to try to disguise it.

He was wise to the finagling involved in keeping parents in the dark, his own adolescent failings a far sight lower than tobacco.

Snake low, belly on the ground low, in the dirt low.

If his daughter's worst was sneaking a smoke, and if Bobby's worst was smoking or drinking or even flirting with another girl, Reece could still grip the boy's hand and congratulate him as the son-in-law he felt in his bones Bobby was bound to be. Everyone was entitled to keep secret a little to himself, and DruAnn was a girl wanting to draw you all out, every bit. Reece did not let her bore him down to bedrock with her questions, for no good could come of confessing facts that let loose pent-up harm. Bobby'd have to learn it didn't pay to give over everything.

In his own youth, Reece had pulled the wool over plenty of eyes that watched him close. He did it out of spite and to show he didn't need surveillance but the bumper evidence summer of '78 still and ever haunted him.

His dad was a tough detective, even if his day job was hopping up and down out of a truck, delivering milk as part of the last-leg-home-delivery from Mahlmer's Dairy. He was always on Reece's case, an insistent weight pressing in the same way a washerwoman bears her iron down on a cotton shirt, driving on about lawlessness and how it would catch up with a man. You wouldn't guess an ordinary milkman had so much Dick Tracy in him.

These days everybody got their milk from Kroger or Walmart and had to drive twenty miles to I-75 over at

Georgetown, but most did it without complaint.

Paris, Kentucky had nothing but 7-Eleven, where they hiked up the price because they had you over a barrel if you were in there buying milk in the first place. You needed it right then, you forked over the dough.

No one had the luxury of home delivery, cream at the bottle's top under the paper lid, the quarts in glass and stored in a metal box at the doorstep, ready for children's cereal or a morning's cup of coffee.

Reece was no milkman, only a milkman's son whose fortunes lay in insurance, a hard-to-define subject. His father managed to dismiss the profession because he couldn't see a concrete thing attached to it – no truck or tool or item produced by manufacturing. Reece tried to meet him halfway.

He said, "All progress rests on the word *if* and the gamble you're willing to take."

"Piss-poor explanation," his dad said. "Risk-averse flimflam."

Answering the old man's questions had never been easy, from present day and casting all the way back to that first cross-examination at seventeen that cut him down to size.

You can't explain something like that away, son." His dad, ready to hear an excuse and ready to dismiss it just as quick.

Reece had turned his back a split second after he'd gunned out of the narrow lane behind the Farmer's Tobacco Warehouse, two blocks from Angilo's Pizza. Even a one-horse town like Paris had rundown streets, its share of questionable folk – transients, the lawless and plain bums who propped up and perpetuated patches of seaminess the church women worked at eradicating. Former arteries for tobacco commerce had eroded into alleys little used other than for travel-through.

"What were you doing over there, for Christ's sake?" His dad and his third degree.

After loading pizzas for five hours, Reece was taking a short-cut, in a rush to a girl, to Samantha, who'd promised him something special if he could make it to her by midnight, and his imagination was cooking like the ovens he'd been working all night.

He didn't see the kid dart from between parked or abandoned cars up and down both sides like stalled traffic. Boy or girl, maybe neither, maybe a dog, dark fur or dark clothes, coyote at the edge of his eye, loping. His foot pushed pedal – which pedal? – the suddenness scared the shit out of him. He wasn't sure if he hit gas or brake.

"Kids out after midnight got no business." His father's misplaced righteousness.

"I wasn't speeding," Reece said. "I wasn't going more than fifteen."

"Who saw you?"

So his dad was asking for witnesses? Reece shrugged. He didn't even see what he thought he saw, what he thought he bumped, in that alley. His mother's cuckoo clock chimed one, two rooms away. Samantha said she'd wait, but she'd probably given up.

"Nobody saw you? Nobody stopped you?"

"Well, I didn't wait around." Even to his own ears, Reece sounded whiny and indignant

Where's the regret, son? His father didn't speak. Only he'd mouthed the question so much in the past, Reece had developed telepathy on the subject.

Regret. Reece had been walling it up and heading it off and doing an end-run around it even, since something kissed the front bumper, hummed along the driver's side panel, tugged the steering wheel right out of his pizza-smelling hands.

Regret, at the same time, coming up through the car's floor, so it shocked the brake pedal, sent his toes tingling and punching down, STOP, SWITCH, twist the wheel, reverse, cut, gear to drive, gun it. All instinct and reflex, not a whit of consciousness or conscience attached. He didn't remember driving home, but the car cooled in the garage like a well-ridden horse.

He faced-up his dad, ready for meltdown, curses, maybe even the strap. But cool, man, Reece had been ice, ready to take it, whatever *it* was, and his dad ate up his boy's calm. The house, and his dad's response, were both eerily quiet.

Puzzling that once Reece hinted at some kind of confession, his dad swept it under the rug. Floodgates inside him readied to burst with the adrenaline that surged and pooled. He was sweating, he was going to cry, he might even piss his pants.

"Let's check out the Charger." His dad turned his back on the regret he'd just demanded. Silently or with words, his method had the same intent: To ruffle Reece, to batter-ram him if he had to, to take him down where he stood and gloat over how easy it had been. Reece, frozen and awash in regret, didn't know how to get rid of it.

His father slapped him across the face, which helped some.

"The fear that's rising up in you, pinch it off right now. No time for it." His dad was a fickle son-of-a-bitch.

They slipped out the kitchen to the attached garage.

The door's spring screeched loud enough, but Mother, she slept through. And what bumped in the night, could be dead or dying or off in the woods licking its wounds. It could be animal, vegetable, mineral. Maybe somebody threw a stone or a piece of log, a two by four, dumpster garbage. It didn't have to be alive, so it didn't have to be dead.

"The Charger's headlight's busted."

"I'll pay for it."

"You bet you will." His dad sucked air through his teeth, whistled. "And there's blood."

Reece's stomach curdled, all those belly juices working overtime on the crust and sauce and dregs of pizza from the late supper he'd stuffed down at Angilo's between turning the pies and racking them in the oven. His legs went AWOL and he had to lean against the car to keep standing. Tears beat at the toughness he strove for.

"No use crying over spilled milk." That, from a milkman. "Man's got to face the consequences of his accident."

"You mean actions."

"I mean accident." He couldn't have made *accident* sound more iffy.

"I wasn't drinking," Reece said. An unopened six-pack he'd swiped from Angilo's refrigerated case was turning lukewarm under the front seat.

Shit, he'd been just a kid then and instead of taking the car keys, or beating him senseless or tearing him verbally up one side and down the other, or calling the police, his dad had cast him in an absurd play that exacted no revenge and demanded no contrition, peppered him with skewed questions that never got to the heart of the accident. Which it was, an accident. Unexplained and unexamined results chewed at Reece from the inside. They covered it up. And the law never came.

All that supposing, with no concrete answers. Criminal or not, twenty years later, he still couldn't say.

Just days after the accident, he'd already changed so much his friends shook their heads as they drifted and gave him distance. Reece, he's gone loony, man.

He didn't call Samantha or give a reason why he'd dropped her. Once, she'd isolated him in a Stolefield High stairwell after school, grabbed his arm and he just shook her off.

He quit Angilo's without giving fair notice to the old guy, went in, said, "I've got to be out of here, man," and never breathed the carryout's garlicky air again. He gave up eating pizza, and for a while forfeited beer, but repentance had to stop somewhere. All of this a contrived payback to the universe, and even the contrivance, which he meant as some sort of penance, made him feel better than he thought he deserved.

He avoided the warehouse alley and its double-parked cars, though news reports covered no mysterious hit-and-run. Had there not been blood on the headlight, and if his own father hadn't discovered it, Reece half believed his imagination, revving and distracted on his way to Samantha, had overwrought itself and had conjured it, all dream.

Giving up things he loved felt right, well it made him *feel* at least, and he ran full-tilt into a life stripped of all a seventeen-year-old thinks he needs. He quit hunting and hanging with friends at the outlet stores in Georgetown.

He worked on the Charger night and day, perfecting,

in his mind, small imperfections that couldn't be buffed out. He swallowed cheap beer in the quiet of his dad's garage on weekend nights instead of cruising in the gorgeous automobile he babied, the car ticking of its own accord, and the bare overhead bulb sizzling now and then with the threat of giving up. The chamois in his hand felt like a portion of skin he'd somehow peeled off his own person, then folded up and put to work, his pound of flesh.

He paid attention in classes, another hair shirt, part of his transformation, became a straight-A student, surprising his parents and astonishing his Stolefield teachers.

Two houses down the road, Beverly Cummings and her friends tossed flags into the air, working on their timing for the next big halftime show. Red squares of cloth flapped and swirled, as if the girls tossed and caught fire with their pretty hands in their lily-white gloves. Members of the Flag Corp and Beverly, that year's Drum Majorette of Stolefield High. Bev, a girl he'd hardly spoken with, despite seventeen years of growing up near one another. Distance measured more then.

Bev had a majorette's figure she worked hard on achieving and then keeping. Carrying and birthing DruAnn ruined her, she said, but Bev managed to gain back her trimness. Being twenty-one made it hard work, not like when she'd been fifteen and jumping rope so carefree. She said pregnancy possessed her like some sci-fi alien and destroyed her.

"Swear you'll not touch me that way or put me through that ever again," she'd said.

Silly thing to promise, sillier to stick to. But he did, thinking time would soften her stubbornness. His outright begging, drunk or sober, mattered not a whit. The bed they shared was for sleeping. This he accepted, the way a yard dog is quick to learn the length of his tie-out. No use choking over it. Reece learned to live with what was in reach.

He brushed by Bev with his breakfast dishes and when she stepped aside to make room for him, the perfume of the fabric softener she used mixed with her skin's and heavied the slip of air between them. Reece's heart momentarily swam back to the boy he'd been and to Bev's younger self, then just as quickly drawn up like a fish in a net, with the water running off and dying setting in. The dishwater's soap bubbles engaged Bev more deeply than the heat of his legs next to hers.

Evenness, equality, a common ground – they'd had this once, but now they didn't seem to be in the same room without one or the other ceding space and retreating.

Her eyes focused outdoors on the backyard bird feeder, that window above the sink drawing her attention instead of Reece, living and breathing right beside her, which just proved the extent of the disintegration they lived with.

But DruAnn, even mooning over Bobby, she livened up their dull Finch party. Dru was their touchstone, where the two halves of their figure eight intersected and then veered off again. From the day of her birth, DruAnn fascinated and occupied Reece. The fact of her in their world, how he and Bev and the house itself shifted to balance and orbit around her, it all outweighed the claim from his stupid past.

Not to say that his memory wasn't always threatening to pounce and demand wrestling from him. All those alley characters hidden but observant behind the dark glass of parked cars or the shattered windshields of the few burned-out clunkers, they haunted him. Reece, through the years, learned you couldn't outrun what goes bump in the night, what you missed because your head was turned or you were fiddling with the volume on the radio.

You couldn't outrun it because it was burned up in your eyelids. Asleep or awake, it was your vision.

As he'd poured everything into the Charger and walked through the world a passionless robot of a boy, Reece, as a father himself, worked at DruAnn. The kind of life he made, he did it for her. He funnelled his achievements in her direction, even the laughable insurance kudos handed down from the central office. He gave her everything. Why not say it? He spoiled her. He polished her almost and she'd turned out a beauty.

Cars, girls – guys talked about them the same. Ain't she a beaut, a babe, a sweet ride?

A cliché, how girls thought boys fawned over their cars in the very way the girls wished they, too, would be fawned over. But this was different and weird. DruAnn was Reece's baby, and now she was riding around in Bobby Trivette's Charger, as if the classic car itself had u-turned down Memory Lane to prod Reece the way a boy pokes a stick at a piece of roadkill he finds deteriorating in the gravel

Rebel ePublishers
rebelepublishers.com

23486674R00135

Made in the USA
Columbia, SC
10 August 2018